TOAST MORTEM

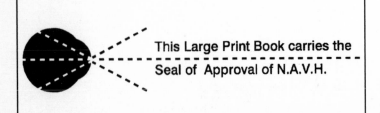

This Large Print Book carries the
Seal of Approval of N.A.V.H.

Toast Mortem

Claudia Bishop

WHEELER PUBLISHING
A part of Gale, Cengage Learning

GALE
CENGAGE Learning™

Detroit • New York • San Francisco • New Haven, Conn • Waterville, Maine • London

LIBRARY OF CONGRESS CATALOGING-IN-PUBLICATION DATA

Bishop, Claudia, 1947–
   Toast mortem / by Claudia Bishop. — Large print ed.
     p. cm. — (Wheeler Publishing large print cozy mystery)
     Originally published: New York : Berkley Prime Crime, c2010.
     "A Hemlock Falls mystery" —T.p. verso.
     ISBN-13: 978-1-4104-3049-6 (pbk.)
     ISBN-10: 1-4104-3049-9 (pbk.)
     1. Hemlock Falls (N.Y. : Imaginary place)—Fiction. 2. Quilliam, Meg (Fictitious character)—Fiction. 3. Quilliam, Quill (Fictitious character)—Fiction. 4. Cooks—Crimes against—Fiction. 5. Cooking schools—Fiction. 6. Sisters—Fiction. 7. Hotelkeepers—Fiction. 8. Murder—Investigation—Fiction. 9. Large type books. I. Title.
   PS3552.I75955T63 2010
   813'.54—dc22   2010026294

Published in 2010 by arrangement with The Berkley Publishing Group, a member of Penguin Group (USA) Inc.

Printed in the United States of America
1 2 3 4 5 6 7 14 13 12 11 10

For Lyn Stanton

CAST OF CHARACTERS

The Inn at Hemlock Falls
Sarah "Quill" Quilliam-McHale owner, manager
Margaret "Meg" Quilliam owner, master chef
Jackson McHale Quill's son
Doreen Muxworthy-Stoker housekeeper, a widow
Dina Muir receptionist and graduate student
Kathleen Kiddermeister head waitress
Mike Santini groundskeeper
Nate the bartender
Elizabeth Chou under chef
Bjarne Bjarnsen under chef
Devon dishwasher
Mallory dishwasher
Max dog
Anson Fredericks guest, member of WARP
Muriel Fredericks guest, his wife
Verena Barbarossa guest, president of WARP

Big Buck Vanderhausen guest, member of WARP

William K. Collier guest, member of WARP

And various waiters, waitresses, and housekeeping staff

The Hemlock Falls Chamber of Commerce

Elmer Henry the mayor

Adela Henry his wife

Marge Schmidt-Peterson local tycoon

Harland Peterson dairy farmer, Marge's husband

Howie Murchinson judge and the village attorney

Miriam Doncaster librarian

Harvey Bozzel advertising executive

Reverend Dookie Shuttleworth minister

Esther West owner, West's Best Kountry Krafts

Nadine Peterson owner, Hemlock Hall of Beauty

And others

The Village of Hemlock Falls

Davy Kiddermeister sheriff

Carol Ann Spinoza animal control officer

Myles McHale Quill's husband, an investigator

Justin Martinez lawyer

And various police officers, storekeepers, farmers, and citizens

Bonne Goutè Culinary Academy

Bernard LeVasque famous chef, author of *Brilliance in the Kitchen*

Madame LeVasque his wife and chief financial officer

Clarissa Sparrow head pastry chef

Raleigh Brewster head of soups and stews

Jim Chen head chef, fish and seafood

Pietro Giancava head chef, sauces, chief sommelier

Mrs. Owens head chef, fruits and vegetables

Bismarck cat

And various waiters, waitresses, and maintenance staff

Supernumeraries

Barstow and Phipps LeVasque's lawyers

Lieutenant Harker a New York state trooper

PROLOGUE

Bernard LeVasque stormed into the kitchen at La Bonne Goutè Culinary Academy in his usual way: his left hand thrust palm out to smack open the swinging doors, his right clenched around his favorite butcher knife. *"Hola!* You collection of *stupides!"* he shouted, by way of greeting.

The academy's five chefs were assembled in the large, airy space.

Despite the fact that M. LeVasque had announced his presence in the same insulting tones for the past three months, all of them reacted with a range of very satisfying behaviors: Pietro Giancava (sauces and wines) hissed like a snake. Raleigh Brewster (soups and stews) let out a muffled shriek. Mrs. Owens (fruits and vegetables) growled like the mastiff she resembled. Jim Chen (seafood and fish) scowled, clenched his fists, and balanced himself evenly on both feet, as if readying to charge his employer.

The only person who remained unruffled was the young and pretty pastry chef, Clarissa Sparrow.

M. LeVasque was pretty sure he could fix that. Mme. Sparrow, he recalled, was the fond owner of Bismarck, the enormous orange-and-yellow cat glowering under the prep sink. Without a word, he strode across the terrazzo floor, grabbed Bismarck by the scruff of the neck, and flung the startled animal out the back door.

Then, with an insincere grin that bared his yellowing teeth, he said, *"Bon matin."*

1

~Courgettes et Tomates~
au Caviar LeVasque
For four *Personnes*

2 medium tomatoes
2 small zucchini
Chopped onion
Chopped parsley
Caviar LeVasque★

Prepare the zucchini and vegetables by slicing in half and scooping out the seeds. Stuff with one cup Caviar LeVasque, garnish with parsley and onion, arrange beautifully.

★Caviar LeVasque is available at my website for a small fee only.
— From *Brilliance in the Kitchen,*
B. LeVasque

"That Mr. Levaskew's going to end up with

his butcher's knife buried smack in the middle of his back one of these days," Doreen Muxworthy-Stoker predicted. "You mark my words."

"Well, it won't be soon enough for me." Meg Quilliam sat curled in the lounge chair farthest away from the outer deck of the gazebo and bit her thumb with a cross expression. Her sister, Quill, sat on that part of the deck that faced the waterfall tumbling into Hemlock Gorge. Doreen, their housekeeper, perched on the sturdy gazebo railing like a broody hen. Jackson Myles Mc-Hale, who was going to be two years old in less than a week, climbed up the shallow steps to the gazebo floor and climbed back down again.

Quill kept a careful eye on her son and wriggled her bare toes in the soft moss that edged the decking.

It was a perfect August afternoon. Sunshine flooded the emerald green lawns surrounding the Inn at Hemlock Falls. Roses and lavender scented the soft air. Flowering clematis, shouting crimson, climbed over the old stone walls of the sprawling building. The breeze that came up from the gorge was cool and smelled of fresh water. Quill didn't want to talk about the horrible Mr. LeVasque. She wanted to roll over in the grass with Jack and tickle him until he collapsed into giggles. But she was a loyal friend and loving sister, so she said: "What's he done now?"

"What's he *done?*" Meg shrieked. "What hasn't he *done!?* He's built a whacking huge cooking academy smack in my backyard and stolen all our customers and you're asking me what's he *done?!*" She wriggled out of the lounge chair, put her hands on her hips, and glared across the gorge.

La Bonne Goutè Academy of Culinary Arts sat on the opposite side of the ravine. It was three stories high. Practically everyone in the village of Hemlock Falls thought it was gorgeous. The building was cream of cream clapboard with hunter green trim. The roof was smooth copper. All three stories were surrounded by clear pine decking. The place was surrounded by apple trees, peach trees, figs, and a vegetable garden that looked as if it belonged outside a French chateau with an army of gardeners at the *duc's* command.

Quill had gone to the open house three months before. Like all the other villagers in Hemlock Falls, she hadn't been able to keep away. She knew that the inside was as serviceable and elegant as the outside. The floors were wide-planked cedar, buffed to a perfect shine. The tasting room was big and dark and cool, and the antique wine racks that covered the walls had come from M. LeVasque's own vineyards in France. As for the kitchens . . . Quill sighed. The biggest classroom had twenty dual-fuel Viking ranges. Four were arranged in each of five stations complete with prep sinks and all the knives, spatulas, graters, sieves, choppers, bowls, measuring cups, ladles, spoons, and whisks an aspiring student chef could ask for.

Hemlock Falls was pleased with the addition of all this glory to their picturesque cobblestone village. Its proprietor, M. Bernard LeVasque, was the author of the best-selling cookbook *Brilliance in the Kitchen.* His television show *The Master at Work* had a successful five-year run on network TV. He attracted tourists in droves.

"I'd like to bomb the place," Meg said through gritted teeth. "I'd like to dump a billion tons of cow manure on that copper roof. I'd like to throw five hundred gallons of brindle brown paint all over that perfect siding."

Jackson Myles McHale glanced up at his aunt, a slight pucker between his feathery eyebrows. The sunshine made his red curls glow like a new penny. He seemed to debate

16

a moment. Then he bent over, grabbed the red plastic shovel Quill had bought for him so he could dig in the dirt like Mike the groundskeeper, and presented it to Meg. "Frow this!" he said, with a pleased expression. "Frow it *now.*"

"Thuh-row," Quill corrected gently. "Thuh-thuh-thuh. Thuh-row, Jack."

"Frow," Jack said ecstatically. "Frow, frow, frow!"

"Give it here, Jack," Meg demanded. "And I'll throw it right up M. LeVasque's . . ."

Quill cleared her throat noisily, then extracted the shovel from her son's chubby grasp and sat on it. "No throwing," she said firmly. "Either one of you. And M. LeVasque is undoubtedly a grouchy guy, Meg, but let's not talk about this kind of stuff in front of Jack, okay? And for God's sake, don't encourage him to throw things. You'll have to admit," she added, fondly, "that he's the smartest little boy and he picks up on everything."

"Phooey," Meg said.

"Phooey," Jack echoed. He made a determined effort to extract the shovel from beneath Quill's cotton skirt.

"There, you see?" Quill said. She held the shovel up in one hand. "Darling, you can only have the shovel if you promise not to

17

throw it, okay?"

"Phooey," Jack said. He grabbed the shovel, gnawed at the handle for a bit, and threw the shovel down the steps.

Quill beamed at him. "Get the shovel and bring it back to Mommy, please."

"Phooey," Jack said. "Phooey-phooey-*phooey!*"

"That's enough, young man." Doreen jumped down from the railing and brushed herself off briskly. She wore her usual work uniform of denim skirt, cotton blouse, and canvas shoes. Her gray hair frizzed around her face and the tip of her nose was red from sunburn. Her hands and wrists were gnarled from arthritis and Quill marveled, as she occasionally did, at the toughness in her friend's wiry, seventy-eight-year-old frame. She'd outlived four husbands. Stoker, the last one, had died peacefully in his sleep and left Doreen a comfortably wealthy woman. "That's it. Nap time. Come here to Gram."

"Nap time," Jack said. "No. No. I don't think so."

Doreen bent over with a slight grunt of effort and picked him up. "Say night-night to Mommy." For a long moment, the two pairs of eyes regarded each other; Jack's bright blue and thoughtful, Doreen's black

18

and beady. "Night-night, Gram," he said meekly. Then, suddenly, he yawned widely, put his head on Doreen's shoulder, and went to sleep.

"Amazing," Meg said. They watched the two of them cross the lawn to the Inn. With one hand supporting the toddler's back, Doreen opened the French doors to the Tavern Lounge and disappeared inside.

"It is, isn't it?" Quill sighed. "How come that never works for me?"

Meg turned her head. "You mean Jack and Doreen?" She scowled. "Because you turn into a sap every time you see him. He could stick beans up your nose and you'd think it's adorable. Doreen's over being a sap about kids. She's got how many grand-children of her own?"

"Twenty-two, last count," Quill said. "And that includes Jack, she says. Furthermore, I am not a sap."

"Yes, you are," Meg fumed.

Quill decided not to argue the point. Her sister was the world's best fumer and she'd made it a long-standing practice to ignore the explosions.

Meg clasped her hands behind her back and began to pace. The gazebo was large. Its radius was twenty feet, which Quill knew because she'd designed it herself. And Meg

19

was short, no more than five feet two, even when she was standing on her tiptoes in rage. But the place was too small to accommodate her sister's agitation.

"Here's an idea. Let's go to the beach."

Meg scowled at the gorge. It was a wonderful afternoon, warm, but not sticky, and the air coming up from the Hemlock River smelled like freshly cut grass. The water was a clear greeny brown. From where she stood in the gazebo, Quill could see it lapping peacefully against the little sandy beach she and Mike the groundskeeper had designed together and then installed that spring. Mike had built a sturdy pine staircase on the steep slopes that led down from the Inn, too. The whole thing was quite a hit with the guests. Quill was trying to encourage wisteria to grow around the railings. She'd planted several of the new hybrid hydrangeas at the foot of the stairs, and they were blooming like anything.

On the beach itself, which was small but smoothly sandy, two of the Inn's guests sunned themselves in the pair of Adirondack recliners. Both had sunhats over their faces, but from the brevity of the bikini on the one and the color of the Speedo on the other, it was Mr. and Mrs. Anson Fredericks.

"You mean go swimming? You're trying to change the subject. It's not going to work." Meg started to pace again, her gray eyes narrowed to tiny, glittering slits.

Quill had been trying to change the subject ever since the Bonne Goutè Culinary Academy had thrown open its oversized oak doors in April. Meg came back to it as if scratching at a case of poison ivy.

"You know how many bookings we've got for dinner tonight?"

Three, Quill said silently.

"Three!" Meg roared.

Far down the slope of Hemlock Gorge, Mrs. Fredericks sat up, looked around in a dissatisfied way, and poked her husband in the stomach.

"And it's the *height* of the tourist season. Last year at this time, do you know how many bookings we had the ninth of July?"

Forty-six, Quill said to herself.

"Forty-six!"

Quill sighed.

"And don't you dare try and tell me it's the economy!" Meg stamped to a halt and raised her fists over her head. "If God and the twelve apostles drove up to the Inn in a bus and wanted a room, what would we have to tell him?"

We're full.

"We're *full up!*" Meg flung herself into the wicker rocker next to the little refrigerated bar and pushed herself back and forth with a furious foot. "Oh, no," she said bitterly. "People are coming in droves to the Inn. You and Dina have to beat them off with a stick. But they're not coming for my food. They hate my food. They hate my recipes. They hate me! But the food made by that little jumped up pompous French son of a bi . . ."

Mrs. Fredericks shrieked. It wasn't her breakfast shriek. ("Oh, ew! This is cream? Do you know what kind of fat content is in cream? Don't you people have any soy? Ew!") Or her allergy shriek. ("Oh, ew! Do you know what roses *do* to my sinuses? Ew!")

This was a shriek of terror.

Quill crossed the short distance to the head of the beach staircase in two leaps and was halfway down its length before she pulled herself up and assessed the situation.

Mrs. Fredericks teetered precariously on her Adirondack chair. She waved her hat frantically at a fine, healthy clump of hydrangea. Anson Fredericks had backed into the water. He faced the clump of hydrangea, too. Quill was on the other side of the hydrangea, and from this vantage point, she could see a long, furry orange tail, a plump set of furry orange hindquarters, and two furry ears. The ears were pinned flat against a round hairy head. An ominous, continuous growl had replaced the cheery sound of birdsong.

It was a cat. A very large cat, and it had a bright red bandanna tied around its neck.

Quill started down the steps again.

The hindquarters bunched and the muscles under the glossy coat rippled. Mrs. Fredericks shrieked, "Anson! It's going to jump me!"

After ten years as an innkeeper, Quill was an expert soother. "It's just a cat, Mrs. Fredericks. You can't see him, her, whatever, from here. But I can, and it's just somebody's pet."

"Cat, my ass!" Muriel Fredericks screamed. "It's a goddam panther."

"Bring a gun!" Anson shouted. "We need some kind of gun!"

"A gun?" Quill said, startled.

"Don't move, Muriel! It's probably rabid!" Anson splashed a few feet farther into the river.

Muriel teetered on the edge of the chair and regarded her husband with undisguised contempt. "A fat lot you care, you, you *coward.*"

"It's not going to jump," Quill soothed.

The animal crouched, and its already flattened ears flattened some more. It wriggled its belly into the mulch and flexed its long, sharp claws.

"And if it's going to jump, it's because you're waving your hat around. It thinks you're inviting him to play."

Quill reached the bottom of the steps and regarded the cat a little dubiously. It looked very much like a well-fed domestic tabby except it was much, much, larger. Quill had a good visual sense, and the thing had to weigh forty pounds, at least. "Here, kitty," she said. "Here, kitty, kitty."

"That there's a Maine coon cat." Doreen's voice came from just behind Quill's left ear. She turned around to see that the cavalry had arrived in the form of her sister and her housekeeper. "A what?"

"A Maine coon cat," Doreen explained patiently. "It's one of them big ones."

"It sure is," Meg said, somewhat awed.

The cat turned and regarded the three of them with the sort of confident imperiousness Quill tried to cultivate with her more obnoxious guests. (It never worked.) It growled, drew its lips back over very sharp teeth, and spat. Then it sat up and began to wash its tail with the kind of complete indifference Quill tried to cultivate with cranky food inspectors. (That never worked, either.)

"Well!" Quill said brightly. "You see? It's quite relaxed now that you've stopped waving the hat. I think everything's going to be just fine, Mrs. Fredericks. We've got this under control. Why don't you and your husband go back up to the Inn and relax for a bit in the Tavern Lounge." She looked at her watch. "It's five-ish. You'll be just in time for a nice high tea. Tell Nate the bartender that there'll be no charge."

"More like time for a double martini," Anson Fredericks said as he edged past them.

"Yeah," Muriel said, as she followed him. "And we're due at Bonne Goutè for the Wine Fest at seven. I don't want to spoil it. I think you owe us a few drinks, if you ask me. All that cream and scones stuff is fattening. Not to mention bad for your arteries."

Quill was pretty sure the growling sound wasn't coming from the cat but from her sister, although it was hard to tell. She took a firm grip on Meg's arm and pulled her off the steps and onto the sand. "Martinis, then. Whatever you like."

She didn't watch the Frederickses go but tried to keep a wary eye on both her sister and the cat at the same time, which was difficult, since the cat had retreated farther under the hydrangea. Meg was at the water's edge, throwing fist-sized rocks into the water in a petulant way.

Doreen pushed past Quill, crouched a few feet away from the hydrangea bush and extended her hand. "C'mere, you."

The cat, its front paws folded under its substantial chest, stared at them with the arrogance of a homeboy defending his turf from punks the next street over.

"C'mere, cat." Doreen opened her right hand, which held a revolting-looking gray brown mush. The cat sniffed, sat up, and started to purr like a lawnmower. Then it daintily picked its way through the mulch surrounding the hydrangea and swiped at Doreen's hand. Doreen hollered, dropped the mush, and backed away. The cat smirked and considered the mush. Then it ate it.

"What *is* that stuff?" Quill demanded.

"Liver bits."

"Liver bits?" Quill took a minute to process this. "You carry liver around in your pockets?"

"Jack likes it."

"You feed Jack liver?!"

"Sure."

"Doreen! Liver's an organ meat. It's filled

with cholesterol. It's stuffed with fat. It's horrible stuff."

"A-yuh." Doreen scowled at the cat and looked at the scratch on her hand, which oozed a small bit of blood.

"I don't want you to feed Jack liver bits ever again. Do you hear me?"

Doreen ignored this, as she ignored most of Quill's frequent caveats about the care of her son. "What are we going to do with this here cat?"

"If it were Thanksgiving instead of weeks after the Fourth of July, I could stuff it like a turkey," Meg said. She tossed a final handful of rocks into the river and dusted her hands on her shorts. "It's big enough to feed sixteen."

The cat narrowed its eyes chillingly.

"Just kidding," Meg said. She crouched next to Doreen. "What are we going to do with it? It's too big to tote up the stairs, that's for sure."

"We could call animal control," Quill suggested nervously.

Everybody ignored this, including the cat. Quill was sorry she'd brought it up. The recently appointed animal control officer was Carol Ann Spinoza, who had lost her cushy job as the village of Hemlock Falls' meanest tax assessor and was now the vil-

27

lage's meanest dog catcher.

"We'll put up a notice in the post office," Quill said. "And maybe your friend Arthur can publish its picture in the *Gazette*, Doreen, if that's okay with you. It's obviously somebody's pet."

They all looked at the red bandanna, which was neatly ironed and carefully tied.

"And I'm sure that its owner is searching frantically for it," Quill added.

Meg looked dubious. Quill wasn't too sure of it, herself. But Doreen nodded and scooped another handful of liver bits from her pocket. The cat looked up at her with calculating interest and came out into the sunshine.

"And we'll bring food down for it, that's what we'll do." Quill pulled her cell phone from her pocket. Myles had given her a new one at Christmas and she'd painfully learned all the applications, so she could take pictures of Jack to send to his father. Myles had been on assignment in the Middle East for four months, and if she stopped to think about it, she couldn't bear it. So she took picture after picture and texted them off, and it helped, a little, but not really enough. She peered through the little viewfinder and said, "Can you guys move him away from the flowers?"

"Not me," Meg said flatly. "He's still mad about the turkey comment."

Doreen laughed scornfully and sucked the scratch mark on the palm of her hand.

"Never mind, then." Quill backed up a few feet. "I'm just trying to compose a better shot. The thing is, that red bandanna looks positively dire with that orange coloring, and the whole thing clashes with the blue hydrangea." The silence was marked. Quill looked up from the viewfinder. "What?!"

"Just take the shot," Meg said. "Yes, you are an artist. And yes, you've got an oil hanging at MoMA. And yes, countless critics have applauded your — what was the phrase in *Art Today*? Your preternatural sense of color. But."

"But?"

"That cat's a menace," Doreen said. "We gotta get the word out, or next thing you know it's going to be eating the guests. If you don't take the picture, I will. Besides, that there bandanna might help with identification." She snorted. "And who's going to give a rat's behind about the color of them hydrangeas?"

"I don't know if the bandanna's going to make all that much difference. That's a one-of-a-kind cat, that is," Meg observed.

29

"Will you guys stand next to it, then? I need a reference point so people can see how big it is."

Meg flatly refused, on the grounds that the cat would just as soon bite her as look at her. Doreen didn't bother to reply to this suggestion at all, although she scattered some of the liver bits under the bush to tempt the animal farther into the sunshine.

Meg clicked her tongue impatiently. "Come on, Quill. Hurry up. I've got to get to the kitchen and prep for all three of the stupendous meals I'm making tonight. And you've got that executive session for the Chamber of Commerce at five o'clock, don't you?"

Guiltily, Quill looked at her watch again. She'd be late for the executive session. She sighed, moved the cell phone up and down and crosswise, and shot five really bad photos of the cat. Then she took the rake they always left by their little beach and neatened the sand up and they all trooped back up the stairs.

Bismarck ate the rest of the liver bits. He stretched, yawned widely, and retired under the hydrangea bush to plot revenge against the Frenchman.

2

~ASPERES VINAIGRETTE~
FOR FOUR *PERSONNES*

16 stalks young asparagus
Vinaigrette LeVasque*

Poach the asparagus lightly in salted water. Drain. Arrange beautifully on plates. Dribble the Vinaigrette LeVasque over the stalks in an attractive way. Eat with the fingers, *non?*

*Vinaigrette LeVasque is available at my website for a small fee only.
— From *Brilliance in the Kitchen,*
B. LeVasque

Marge Schmidt-Peterson squinted at the tiny picture of the cat on Quill's cell phone and shook her head. "Don't think I've seen it around. It's a big sucker, though." Marge, a local businesswoman, and the richest person in Tompkins County, was the Chamber treasurer. She passed the camera on to Elmer Henry.

Elmer, mayor of Hemlock Falls and current president of the Hemlock Falls Chamber of Commerce, took a long, earnest look and said, "I do believe I have seen that animal somewhere."

"Really?" Quill said hopefully. She was the Chamber secretary and, due to a certain amount of absentmindedness when it came to taking notes, not a very good one. She was reelected each year under protest. Hers.

"Can't bring it to mind, though." He passed the camera on to Harland Peterson, a local dairy farmer who'd been elected vice president because Marge Schmidt-Peterson had married him last year, and she wanted it that way. Harland was chewing a toothpick. He shifted the toothpick from one side of his mouth to the other and said, "We got a calf about the size of that thing, Margie. But none of 'em are missing, as far as I know."

"Cat or no cat, we got to get down to business," Elmer said briskly.

"Right," Marge said, with a heavy emphasis that didn't bode well for a fast-moving meeting. "It's about those damn parking meters in front of my restaurants."

Elmer sighed. "We've been over this before, Marge. The board of supervisors voted 'em in, and they're going to stay right where they are."

"You know how many of my customers are bellyaching about those meters?"

"I know," he said huffily, "because you keep calling my office and bellyaching about them yourself. All I have to say to you is that they're bringing much-needed income to this town, and anyone who complains about helping those kids out at the high school . . ."

"Who's complaining about helping the kids at the high school?"

"You are! Those parking meter funds can be used for extra textbooks, extra computers, what have you."

"Could be? Or actually are?"

Elmer hunched his shoulders. "Soon. Anyways, you're just a plain bad citizen, Marge, to take textbooks away from the hands of those high schoolers. Besides," he added, "it isn't all that much, when you come right down to it. You got a bunch of cheapskates there at your diner, Marge. Not my fault if they aren't willing to part with a few quarters to eat at your place."

"Textbooks," Marge repeated.

"They can be used for that, yes, sir." Elmer's sigh would have done credit to Saint Sebastian facing the arrows. After a short — and on Marge's part, disconcerted, silence — he waved the official gavel, and finding nowhere convenient to whack it, shifted grumpily in his chair. "How come we're squashed in here like this, Quill?"

Quill's office was located just past the front door to the Inn, behind the reception desk. When it was occupied by three comfortably sized citizens of Hemlock Falls, it seemed to have too much furniture. Marge and Harland sat together on the three-cushioned couch, which was patterned in heavy chintz printed with bronze chrysanthemums. Quill sat behind her desk, which was made of cherry and in the Queen Anne style. Elmer sat at the small Queen Anne table, which was totally covered by the coffee service and a plate of Meg's sour cream scones.

"I'm sorry it's a little crowded," Quill said. "The group we have here booked the conference room every day this week."

"They got a meeting at five o'clock in the afternoon?" Elmer said. "I saw most of 'em in the Tavern Lounge knocking back booze when I came in. If they're not meeting in there right this minute why are we stuck in this place?"

"They don't want anyone in there," Quill said. "Not even the cleaning staff. They lock it when they aren't inside."

Marge pursed her lips. "What kind of group would that be?"

Quill hesitated. Marge generally put people in mind of one of those short, aggressive tanks that had been so successful in Iraq (although marriage to Harland had mellowed her a bit), which made ducking her interrogations somewhat hazardous. "It's called WARP."

"WARP?"

"Like *Star Trek*," Quill said, somewhat obscurely.

"It's some kind of rehab program," Elmer said. "One of those twelve-step jobbers."

Quill blinked. She thought about asking Elmer why in the world he thought that, but didn't. Everybody had what they thought was an informed opinion in a town the size of Hemlock Falls.

"Drunks," Elmer said comprehensively. "And you let 'em in the Tavern bar?"

"They aren't drunks," Marge said. "They don't look like drunks or act like drunks. And even if they were drunks, it's none of your business, Elmer."

Quill, who thought that drinkers came in all shapes and sizes and couldn't be pigeonholed, had to agree that it wasn't anyone's business whether the WARP people drank all the gin in Tompkins County. Although if WARP's bar bill was anything to go by, it had to be the most unsuccessful twelve-step program ever.

Marge pinned Quill with a steely gaze. "Looks like they got quite a bit of money to throw around. Why don't you bring them on down to the Croh Bar for Happy Hour sometime this week?"

"Insurance business is a bit slow," Harland said, by way of explanation. "Margie's not one to pass up a good prospect."

"Oh. Well." Quill cleared her throat. Marge was perfectly capable of marching down the hallway to the Tavern Lounge and shaking Big Buck Vanderhausen by the scruff of the neck until he coughed up a premium on his dually. "When the organizers booked the rooms, they stressed the confidential nature of their group," she said apologetically. "And they especially asked about how private we were here at the Inn." Then, because she wasn't certain what she had to apologize for, she added firmly, "I'm not sure that it's a recovery program. They seem to be interested in small business. They asked me to give them a talk on how to run a bed-and-breakfast, for example."

"This isn't a bed-and-breakfast," Marge said with a dangerous look in her eye. "And if they want to know anything about running a small business, why didn't you tell them about me?"

"You don't want to talk about business with a bunch of drunks," Elmer said patiently.

"They aren't drunks," Quill said.

"Kayla Morrison found the Serenity Prayer in a wastebasket in that room two-twenty-five of yours," Elmer said. "Told me so herself."

Kayla was a new hire in housekeeping and clearly needed a reminder about the innkeeper's number one rule: no gossiping. Although, come to think of it, not gossiping wasn't as important as not belting the guests, so it'd have to be the number two rule.

"Serenity Prayer. Rehab. Stands to reason," Harland said thoughtfully. "Drunks, huh?"

"I wouldn't call the existence of the Serenity Prayer any kind of evidence at all, Elmer. Lots of people find the Serenity Prayer very soothing."

Elmer looked smug. "Drunks, for example."

"Look at the Irish," Quill said. "You'll find

a copy of that prayer in every pub in Ireland."

"Like I said. Dru . . ."

"Shut up, Elmer," Marge said. "We've got enough troubles without you insulting the Irish. You planning on getting this meeting going anytime soon?"

"I have enough trouble with you insulting *me,*" Elmer said, with a certain amount of dignity.

The meeting descended into a squabble, a regular Chamber practice, and Quill drifted into a brief reverie.

The precise nature of the WARP group puzzled her a little, if only because none of the members were at all alike. A recovery program was a reasonable explanation for the wildly disparate personalities, so Elmer might be half right. The very urban Fredericks huddled in earnest conversation with Mrs. Barbarossa (seventy-two and a cross-stitching grandmother), who in turn spent most mornings with Big Buck Vanderhausen from Lubbock, Texas (forty-six and an expert in long-haul trucking). And then there was the odiously unctuous mortgage banker William Knight Collier, who had an *America for Americans!* sticker on his car. What all these people had in common she couldn't imagine.

"Anyway!" Elmer whacked the gavel on the table leg. "I call this executive session of the Hemlock Falls Chamber of Commerce meeting to order. And if you can keep your opinions to yourself for a change, Marge Schmidt, I'd appreciate it."

"Peterson," Marge barked.

"Huh?"

Marge tapped the very large diamond on her ring finger with an admonitory air.

"Yeah, well. Whatever. Quill? You got the minutes from the last meeting?"

Quill gave a guilty start and patted the side pockets of her skirt. She pulled out her sketch pad (which was filled with charcoal drawings of Jack), a couple of tissues, the flash card for her cell phone, and a small tube of sunscreen. No minutes. She tugged at her hair and thought a minute. Since Myles's assignment overseas was to last six months or more, she had moved out of their small cobblestone house and back into her old suite on the third floor of the Inn. She was pretty sure the minutes were on top of Jack's clean diapers upstairs. Or maybe not.

"We don't need the minutes," Marge said, after a swift appraisal of Quill's thoughtful face. "This is an executive session, and we're here to approve the budget for the Welcome Dinner. We only need the minutes if we've got a full chamber meeting, and this isn't it."

"Lucky for us," Elmer grumbled. "We'd be squashed like sardines if the full Chamber was to meet in here."

Quill flipped to a clean page in her sketch pad. "Ready!" she said brightly.

"Finally!" Elmer said. "Okay, Margie. What we have is this amazing chance to offer a great big welcome to the best thing that's hit this town since I don't know what."

"Since the Colonel Cluck's Fried Chicken hut, maybe?" Marge asked sarcastically. "Or maybe MacAvoy's famous nudie bar? Or the Church of the Rolling Moses?"

These references to past civic disasters failed to ruffle Elmer's spirits. "I mean the Bon Gooty culinary place," he said patiently. "You missed the last Chamber meeting, on account of Harland's cows calving all at once, but we decided to give M'ser LeVasque a hearty how-do at Chamber expense." (Under stress, Elmer's Kentucky origins were obvious in his speech.)

Marge rolled a startled eye in Quill's direction. "We did?"

"We did," Quill said. "Since the culinary academy opened up, tourist revenues have gone up by . . . by . . ." She flipped through the sketch pad, in fruitless search for her notes on the exact percentage. "By a lot," she finished.

"The man's a genius." Elmer's expression of solemn respect nettled Marge, who grunted in a derisive way. But she said, reluctantly, "You might be right about that. He's got out-of-towners flocking to that place. And when we get tourists, everyone benefits. I hear the resort's booked through the summer. The Marriott down on Route 15 is doing well, too." She swiveled her head and eyed Quill. "Even you guys are full up these days. And it's all students and people wanting to slurp down wine and stuff their faces with this so-called gourmet food at Bernie's academy." She sucked reflectively on her lower lip. "Both my restaurants are doing okay, too, despite those damn parking meters. People's guts need a rest from the fancy stuff." Marge's partner, Betty Hall, was in charge of both the All-American Diner (Fine Food! And Fast!) and the popular Croh Bar. Meg claimed that Betty was the best short-order cook in the eastern United States.

"Exactly," Elmer said. "Everybody's doing right well by this fellow."

Marge's steely gaze narrowed a touch. "Except Meg. Way I hear it, you got people stayin' here at the Inn, but they ain't eating here at the Inn."

Nobody looked at Quill.

"Yeah," Elmer said. "Well, that's true. The way I see it, there's a limit to how much gourmet food a body can take. You've got to take the bitter with the sweet, I always say. Anyhow!" He thumped the gavel against the chair leg, but since everyone in the room was paying attention to him already, it seemed quite superfluous to Quill, who was smarting a little at the cavalier dismissal of her sister's concerns. "So here's the thing. We're giving M'ser LeVasque a thank-you from the town this Friday."

"How much of a thank-you?" Marge asked.

Elmer addressed the air over his head. "Hello? Excuse me? Is this why we're having an executive session here?" He lowered his gaze and looked just past Marge, concentrating on the oil painting hanging over the couch. Quill had painted it twelve years ago, just after she and Meg had purchased the Inn. The two sisters sat on the banks of the gorge, with the waterfall behind them. "I just got the numbers from M'ser LeVasque, and all we have to do is vote approval of the budget . . ."

Marge leaned forward and clapped a

meaty hand on Elmer's thigh. "Hang on a second. You got numbers from who? And for what?"

"A select dinner of the town's most important officials." Elmer slipped an envelope out of his shirt pocket. "LeVasque says he won't cook for more than thirty people, though. So we have to keep the invite list pretty quiet. I got the menu and the budget right here." He waved the envelope in the air. Marge grabbed it, removed the contents, smoothed it out on her knee. She looked up at Elmer and glowered.

There was a short silence.

"This would be you and Adela, attending this here dinner," Marge said. Something in the tone of her voice reminded Quill of the very aggressive cat under the hydrangea bush outside.

Elmer nodded. "And you and Harland, of course, and Howie and Miriam."

"The town justice and the village librarian," Marge said. Since everyone in the room knew perfectly well who Howie Murchison and Miriam Doncaster were, Quill knew Marge was making a point. But where Marge was headed was anybody's guess.

"Who else?" Marge demanded. "Dookie and them?"

Quill fiddled with her pencil. Then she

43

started a quick sketch of a scowling Marge holding a panicked Elmer upside down by his heels. When Marge's grammar started to deteriorate, you knew she was annoyed.

"Of course, the Reverend and Mrs. Shuttleworth will be invited," Elmer said. "Most of the Chamber members. Thing is, he won't cook for more than thirty people, being a particular person, so we won't be able to have all of the Chamber members there."

"That's it?"

"That's it."

"We've got twenty-four members, and that doesn't count the spouses. How are you picking and choosing?"

Elmer ran a finger under his shirt collar. "We have to decide that at this meeting. I was thinking that maybe you . . ."

Marge's laugh was exactly like a pistol shot. "I'm supposed to pick out nine Chamber members and tell them we're spending a ton of town money for a dinner by the best chef in the United States of America and they ain't invited?"

"Well," Elmer said feebly.

"And where is this banquet supposed to go on?"

"At Bonne Goutè, of course."

Marge hunched forward, forearms on her

knees, her teeth inches from Elmer's face. "I'm looking at a bill that's a hundred dollars a plate for thirty people. And that don't include the drinks. Who's paying for this, Elmer?"

"The town, of course," Elmer said. "You know how much money we're making from those parking meters?"

3

~CONFITURE DE TOMATES ROUGE~

6 pounds medium-sized red tomatoes
4 1/2 pounds finely ground sugar
Zest of lemon rind plus juice

Slice tomatoes, remove seeds, slice thinly, and arrange in large glass bowl. Sprinkle sugar attractively over all. Let sit for twenty-four hours. Cook over low heat for two hours after adding lemon seasoning. Cool. Spoon into sterilized jars and label.*

*Your personalized home-cooking jar labels may be purchased from my website.

— From *Brilliance in the Kitchen,*
B. LeVasque

"What was the ruckus out front half an hour ago?" Meg stood at the birch prep table in her big kitchen, a cleaver in one hand and a clump of cilantro in the other. "Somebody get attacked by bees?"

"Marge got mad at the mayor." Quill settled into the rocking chair by the cobblestone fireplace and propped her feet up on the cast-iron fender. "And then the mayor got mad at Marge. And then Harland Peterson settled it by yelling the loudest. And then everyone went home."

"That was all the car doors slamming." Meg began whacking the cilantro into little pieces. "Now, in better times" — whack! — "I couldn't have heard a thing" — whack! — "because my kitchen would be full of the happy sound of two sous-chefs prepping for dinner, the pot person scrubbing pots, and the bus person scrubbing the sinks." Whack! Whack! Whack! "But, as you can see, I'm here in glory all by my silent lonesome." She scooped up the bits and dropped them into a stainless-steel bowl. Then she folded her arms and glared at her sister.

Quill set the rocker going with a shove of her foot. "At least we didn't have to lay anyone off. We're always full for breakfast. And lunches aren't too bad. And the dishwasher and the prep person will be in pretty soon."

"How long do you think Bjarne and Eliz-

47

abeth are going to hang around making scrambled eggs and rye toast?"

Both sous-chefs had been with Meg for years, and were fiercely jealous of the Inn's reputation. They were even fiercer about their own reputations in the notoriously competitive world of gourmet cooking.

Meg correctly interpreted Quill's look of dismay. "They're professionals, for cripes's sake. They need a challenge. And don't even *hint* that breakfast can be as difficult as dinner."

"Lunch . . ." Quill ventured.

"Hah. Lunch is day-trippers and campers wanting macaroni and cheese."

This was true. Quill cast a wistful look around the kitchen. The twelve-burner Viking stove was polished to its usual brilliant sheen. A twelve-gallon pot of water simmered on one of the back burners, with a comfortably familiar sound. The herbs and spices hanging from the oak beams overhead scented the air with sage, thyme, and garlic. From her seat by the fireplace, she could see the vegetable garden out back, overflowing with early August bounty: tomatoes, green beans, cucumbers, onions, yellow squash, and manically over-productive zucchini. Meg had added edible flowers to her herb garden a few years back, and there was a glimpse of the bright orange reds of nasturtiums beyond the wire fence Mike had put up to keep out the rabbits. It was homey and beautiful. But it wasn't as slick as the kitchens and gardens at Bonne Goutè. It wasn't even close.

Meg grabbed a colander of ripe tomatoes, marched to the stove, and dumped the fruit into the pot.

"Gazpacho?" Quill guessed, hopefully.

"Maybe," Meg said crossly. "Maybe I'm getting them nice and soft so I can pitch them at Bernard LeVasque the next time he sets foot in my kitchen." She grabbed the pot, marched to the sink, and drained the tomatoes back into the colander. Then she began to peel them with her bare fingers. Meg's hands looked like most professional chefs' — calloused and scarred with knife cuts — but Quill still couldn't figure out why she never seemed to feel the heat of things like parboiled tomatoes. Then what Meg had just said registered and she said, "What? LeVasque's been in your kitchen?"

"Yep."

"When!"

"Just after lunch."

"Just after lunch?" At least that explained Meg's ill humor out in the gazebo. "And he's gone now?"

"Unless Mike ran him over in the kitchen parking lot."

Quill got up, went to the back door, which was open on this pleasant summer afternoon, and peered outside. All she saw was her dog, Max, stretched peacefully under the balcony that ran across the back of the building. The only cars in the lot were her battered Honda, Meg's old pickup truck, and a rusty Ford Escort that probably belonged to a friend of Mike the groundskeeper. She came back inside and tugged at her hair. Quill's hair was red and wildly springy and it suffered a lot from her emotional states. She perched on one of the stools at the prep station. "So tell me what happened."

"Offered me a job," Meg said briefly. "Figured I had some time on my hands and could use the extra work."

"Oh, my." Quill shot a glance at the wall where the sauté pans were neatly arrayed by size. The eight-incher was still in place and didn't seem to be dented. Meg usually chose the eight-incher when she was in the mood to make her point in a forceful way.

Meg followed her gaze and said, "Nope . . . I didn't chase him out of here with that."

"Then what?" Quill asked, rather hollowly.

Meg nodded at the knife rack. The largest butcher's cleaver hung slightly askew.

"Yikes," Quill said.

"That fathead," Meg said without heat. "Thought he'd come here to crow, but I fixed his little red wagon."

"You didn't actually hit him or anything," Quill said.

Meg rolled her eyes. "Have I ever, in all my life, actually inflicted physical harm on another person?"

"Bobby DeRitter, in fourth grade," Quill said promptly. "You pulled a fistful of hair right out of his tiny little head."

"Okay. Excepting Bobby DeRitter. Who deserved it, by the way."

"No," Quill admitted. "You throw stuff around. You holler. But I'd have to say, it's basically stress relief. So you just waved the butcher's cleaver at LeVasque."

"I may have given LeVasque a different impression," Meg admitted. "I may have intimated that the garden out back is the repository for a number of people who've incurred my disapproval, and I may have suggested that I was ready to add to their number."

"A-*hum*," Quill said.

"So we may be getting a visitor."

"A visitor?"

The screen door at the back slapped open and closed.

First in was Max, Quill's dog. If Tompkins County ever ran an ugly dog contest, Max would win hands down. His coat was mostly to blame for his raffish appearance. It was a strange mixture of gray, ochre, tan, scruffy white, and flecks of black. One ear flopped over his left eye. The other stood straight up. At some point in his bohemian past, he'd broken his plumelike tail, and it drooped in a desultory way over his hindquarters.

Behind Max was Davy Kiddermeister, the village sheriff. Quill was pretty sure that the clench in her stomach wasn't due to her need for some food, but to the official-looking document Davy held in his hand and the blush that turned his normally pink cheeks bright red. Davy was Kathleen Kiddermeister's younger brother. Kathleen was the Inn's most loyal waitress, and every time the Quilliam sisters ran afoul of the sheriff's department (a frequent occurrence, due mostly to Meg's and Quill's misguided efforts at amateur detection) Kathleen gave Davy what for. It looked like Davy was dreading his sister's wrath once again.

"Oh, dear," Quill said. "Just tell me nobody's dead."

"Nobody's dead. Somebody's pissed off, though. Sorry. But I've got to lay this on Meg, here." He waved the document in the air. When neither Quill nor Meg moved forward to take it, he straightened up, walked over to Meg, and said sternly, "Margaret Quilliam?"

"Phuut!" Meg said.

"I hereby serve you this summons and complaint." He grabbed her hand and folded her tomato-stained fingers over it. "Sorry about that. Sometimes it's rough, having to perform official duties. I know you won't hold it against me."

Meg shrugged. "Whatever."

He added hopefully, "Got anything to eat?"

"Give me that." Quill leaned over and grabbed the summons.

Meg relinquished the paper without comment. "Liver pâté with stone-ground mustard. And some pretty good goat salami." She moved to the meat refrigerator and took out a couple of plastic containers. "Some blueberries, maybe?"

"Thanks," Davy said gratefully. He eased himself onto a prep stool. "Been on traffic patrol all day and I missed lunch."

"This says you threatened to kill Bernard LeVasque," Quill said. "At least, I think that's what it says. *Threat of grievous bodily harm, assault . . .* battery is actually whacking somebody, right? Assault's the threat. So there's no allegation of actual injury. Thank goodness for that." She folded the paper into neat thirds. "Argh. Argh. I suppose I'd better call Howie Murchison."

"Got a warrant, too," Davy said through a mouthful of pâté. "Sorry."

"A warrant? For Meg's arrest?!"

"Yep. Sor—"

"Stop," Quill said. Then, patiently, she continued, "Did anyone actually see this alleged assault? I mean, if it's just Meg's word against LeVasque's, there's no independent proof."

"Yep."

"Please don't talk with your mouth full, Davy." There were many advantages to being the fond mother of a two-year-old. Chief among them was Quill's newly discovered ability to make polite demands. "And 'yep,' it's just LeVasque's unsubstantiated word, or 'yep,' there's a witness?"

The swinging doors to the dining room banged open, and Dina Muir, Quill's best (and only) receptionist walked in. She was followed by a slim, pretty brunette, who looked vaguely familiar.

Dina bent a purposeful eye on the platter

of blueberries and headed over to the prep counter. "Hey, Quill. Hey, Meg." She gave Davy a pleased smile. "And what are you doing here? We're still on for the movies tonight, I hope?"

"Yep."

Quill resisted the impulse to yank the liver pâté away from Davy and dump it into the disposal, along with the fistful of blueberries Dina was cramming into her mouth.

Dina's long brown hair was drawn back in a jaunty ponytail. She adjusted her red-rimmed spectacles by resettling them on her nose with a forefinger and beamed. "Great. I've been looking forward to the movies all week. It's been a real zoo, here. Those WARP people must have robbed a bank somewhere, and they're trying to spend all their ill-gotten gains at once. Do you know what they're going to do tonight? They ordered *four* stretch limos from . . ."

Quill held up her hand. "Can we talk about this later? We have kind of a situation here." She smiled apologetically at the brunette, who looked anxious. "Hi! I'm Sarah Quilliam."

The brunette nodded and bit her lip. "I know. I mean, I've heard of you. You're the artist, right? I've seen some of your work at MoMA." She stuck out her hand. "I'm Clarissa Sparrow."

"I think I've seen you before," Quill said.

Clarissa looked even more anxious.

"But I can't quite . . ."

"We've got to go," Davy said abruptly. "Thanks for the lunch, Meg. It was great." He stood up and unclipped the handcuffs attached to his belt. "You ready?"

"For cripes' sake," Meg said. "You aren't serious."

"A warrant's a warrant," Davy said. "You give Howie a call, Quill, and we'll get her back on remand in no time, but like I said, we've got to go."

"This is not going to happen," Quill said firmly. "I am not allowing my sister to be dragged off to the county lockup by you or anyone else. For all you know, LeVasque could have made up this whole thing? Where's your proof that my sister threatened to kill him? Where's the witness?"

Davy jerked his thumb in Dina's direction.

Quill whirled and stared incredulously at Dina. Dina paled, bit her thumb, and said, "Oh my God."

"Don't you oh-my-God, me, Dina Muir! You told Davy you saw my sister threaten this bozo?"

"Um," Dina said.

"Um! That's all you've got to say for yourself! Um?!"

"I didn't think . . ."

"You most certainly did *not* think!"

"Oh my God," Dina repeated feebly.

Quill turned back to Davy, who had clipped one handcuff around Meg's wrist and was about to fasten the other. "You get those things off my sister!"

"Thing is," Davy said reasonably, "you can't expect someone like Meg to go quietly."

"She's not going anywhere!"

Davy sighed. "Look. I don't like this any better than you do. But what am I supposed to do here? I've got this warrant. A threat to commit grievous bodily harm is a major felony. I'm supposed to give you guys a break? No way, Quill. I'm sworn to uphold the law." He glanced sidelong at Quill's furious face and said pleadingly, "Now what do you suppose the sheriff would do?"

Clarissa spoke up suddenly. "I thought you were the sheriff."

"He means Myles," Quill said. "My husband. Myles was sheriff of Hemlock Falls when we moved here twelve years ago, and nobody seems to be able to forget it. Including you, Davy. Only now is when you should forget that you are. Sheriff, that is. As for what Myles would do." She grabbed her hair with both hands. "I would not let him arrest my sister!"

Davy gave Meg a gentle nudge toward the back door. "Call Mr. Murchison. As soon as I have a legal remand order, I'll bring her right back home. Okay?"

"Meg!" Quill shouted as her sister's slight form disappeared out the back door. "I'll be down to get you out in two seconds."

"Call up Bjarne!" Meg shouted back. "Tell him to save the tomatoes!"

~CAROTTES LEVASQUE~
FOR FOUR *PERSONNES*

2 pounds elegantly small carrots
4 tablespoons olive oil
2/3 cup water
4 tablespoons Paysanne LeVasque⋆
Parsley

Rinse, peel, and slice the carrots. Sauté in olive oil. Sprinkle with sea salt. Cook over low flame for ten minutes, shaking pan occasionally. Add my country spice mix (Paysanne LeVasque) and salt and pepper to taste. Cook covered for twenty minutes. Sprinkle attractively with parsley and serve warm.

*Paysanne LeVasque may be purchased from my website.

— From *Brilliance in the Kitchen,*
B. LeVasque

For a long moment, Clarissa Sparrow, Dina, and Quill just stood and looked at each other. The little impasse was broken by Max, who made an abortive lunge at the remains of the liver pâté on Davy's plate. Dina hauled him off the counter by the scruff of the neck.

"Just give me two seconds here," Quill said. She pulled her cell phone out of her pocket and found Howie Murchison's office number on speed dial. He wasn't in. She glanced up at the kitchen clock. Well after six o'clock. Doreen would be giving Jack his mashed carrots and tofu right about now. And Howie would be at the Croh Bar with Miriam Doncaster.

She tried his cell and got his voice mail message. Then she tried Marge, asked her to call Betty Hall and relay the message to Howie to call her as soon as possible, and set the phone down.

"You," she said to Dina. "You are a rat fink."

Dina put both hands over her face. "Do you think you should call Jerry?" she said, her voice muffled.

"Jerry Grimsby?" Quill glanced up at the clock again. The hands hadn't moved much. Why did she feel as if she'd been stuck in this kitchen filled with lunatics for hours?

"Jerry's restaurant opens at seven for dinner in the summer. He'll be prepping right now."

"Maybe he can get somebody to take her some food or something. Or a file."

Clarissa Sparrow cleared her throat. "Excuse me. Jerry Grimsby? You're talking about the guy who runs L'Esperance over in Ithaca?"

Quill nodded. "He and Meg . . ." She fluttered her hand. "You know."

"He's going to be so pissed off at me," Dina mourned.

"*He* is?" Quill muttered. "I'm not exactly swinging from the chandeliers, here." Her cell phone shrilled the opening bars to "Rondo alla Turca." The little window said *Howie.* Quill picked the phone up as she said, "Go into my office, Dina. Call Bjarne and ask him to cover for Meg here in the kitchen. I'll be with you in a minute."

Howie, thank goodness, wasn't a tut-tutter. But he reminded Quill that he couldn't represent Meg himself, since he'd be the justice called upon to rule on the request for remand. "You know I've taken on a junior partner," he said. In the background, Quill heard the cheerful din that meant Happy Hour at the Croh Bar was in full swing. "His name is Justin Alvarez. I'll

61

send him down to the clink and get things rolling."

She thanked him, shut the cell phone off, and pushed open the doors to the dining room.

One of the three parties that had made dinner reservations was already seated. Quill saw with approval that Kathleen had a tray of drinks ready for them. The couple sat at the table nearest the floor-to-ceiling windows that faced the waterfall. The part of Quill's brain that was perpetually on inn-keeper alert noted that the cadet blue carpeting could probably last another year, and that the deep cream tablecloths really looked very nice with the pale violet blue of the hydrangeas that made up the center-pieces.

Quill waved to Kathleen as she passed by, then paused and greeted the dinner guests. At a guess, they were in their mid-sixties, and from the rose corsage worn by the woman, they had come to the inn for a celebration.

"Welcome to the Inn at Hemlock Falls," Quill said warmly. "Is this your first time with us?"

They nodded. "Couldn't get in at Bonne Goutè," the woman said. "And it's our fortieth wedding anniversary. Well, it's tomorrow, actually, and the kids have this big party planned, but I said to Frank, wouldn't it be nice if we had dinner, just the two of us?"

"And I said, it sure would," Frank said heartily. "Don't mind being here at all." He waved the menu at her. "It's cheaper than that Bonne Goutè place, too."

"Well," Quill said. "There is that. Kathleen, please see that a bottle of the good champagne's brought to this table will you? And take your time about deciding," she added kindly.

"Little delay in the kitchen," Kathleen offered. She was as sturdily built as her brother, but where Davy Kiddermeister was fair-haired and blushed at the drop of the hat, she was dark-haired and sallow. The only familial resemblance was their pale blue eyes. "Chef's in jail for a bit. But we've got the backup headed this way speedy quick. I'll see to that champagne, Quill."

Quill kept her smile firmly in place as she went through the archway that led from the dining room to the reception area. With luck, the promise of free champagne would keep the fortieth-anniversary couple from scooting out the front door.

Dina wasn't behind the desk. Quill hoped that meant she'd gone into the office with

Clarissa Sparrow and called Bjarne. She noted that the daylilies in the two hip-high Oriental vases that flanked the reception desk were due for a change, looked askance at the spindle with its stack of pink While You Were Out messages, and opened the door to her office with the feeling that this particular day better end soon, or she was going to go stark staring bonkers.

Clarissa Sparrow stood at the window, looking out at the driveway with a hopeful expression. Dina sat on the couch. She straightened up with a guilty start as Quill came into the room and blurted, "Bjarne's on vacation this week. Until Tuesday."

"Oh, no!" Quill sat down behind her desk with a sigh. "I forgot. Oh, phooey."

"And I'm sorry about the stuff with Meg . . . you know. Ratting her out to Davy." She paused, then offered, "Your hair's falling all over a bit."

Quill's hair was always out of control, just like everything else. She pulled it on top of her head in a loose topknot when she got up in the morning, and by this time of day it was always halfway down her back. She twisted it back up and wound the scrunchie twice around the roots. "Well," she said. "Now that I can actually see, things look better."

"I'll quit if you want," Dina said. "It's just that I didn't think! I was in the middle of going over the gestation periods for my copepods and my mind was elsewhere."

"Dina's a graduate student in limnology at Cornell," Quill said in response to Clarissa's puzzled expression. "Limnology's the study of freshwater lakes, which we have plenty of around here, as you know. I don't know what copepods are."

"Lake organisms," Dina said. "A freshwater crustacean of the subclass Copepoda. I keep telling you."

"Whatever," Quill said. "Let's get back to the rat-finkery."

"Well, Davy showed up and I thought he was just, like, asking me about some gossip he'd heard, and then he made me write it out and sign it and I thought, oh, heck. I feel just awful about this! I honestly didn't mean to get Meg into trouble." Two large tears rolled down Dina's cheeks.

"It could be worse," Quill said kindly.

"How?" Dina sobbed.

"Oh, I don't know," Quill said vaguely. "We could be in the middle of a forest fire or something. Here." She pulled a tissue from the box on her desk and leaned over to hand it to Dina. "Look. I've handled the kitchen before, and Doreen is with Jack, as

65

usual, and we only have two other bookings for dinner. So I can cope. There's just that one anniversary couple in the dining room right now. But you'll have to stay on at the reception desk, Dina. No date with Davy."

"That's only fair," Dina said eagerly. "And do you want me to make up a packet to send to Meg? Food and whatever? Some nice soap?"

Quill resisted the impulse to clutch at her hair again. "She'll be back before she needs to take a shower, I'm sure. I called Howie."

"I could give you a hand in the kitchen, if you like." Clarissa Sparrow turned away from the window. "I'm a chef."

"Oh my God," Dina said. "I almost forgot you were there. Quill, this is Clarissa Sparrow. Clarissa, this is my boss, Sarah Quilliam."

"You're a chef?" Quill said. "Of course. Is that where I've seen you before? On the tour of Bonne Goutè?" She closed her eyes, trying to remember. "You're pastry, right?" But there was something else. Clarissa wasn't beautiful, exactly, but she was distinctive. She was slim, maybe too slim, with angular cheekbones, dark hair, and, like Meg, clear gray eyes.

"Right. But I trained at CB . . . Cordon Bleu . . . and I can handle three entrees, no problem."

"That'd be just great," Quill said. "But I hate to impose." She hesitated. "Of course, we'd be glad to reimburse you for your time."

"We'll see," Clarissa said. "It's my awful boss that's put you into this situation, after all. But maybe we can talk about this in the kitchen? I'd better get started."

Quill led the way out of the office and almost collided with Kathleen in the entry-way to the dining room.

"Hi, Quill, hi, Dina." Her gaze slid curiously over Clarissa Sparrow, but she said, "I've been looking for you guys. I gave the VanderMolens another bottle of champagne and a cheese plate, so they're feeling no pain, but the Adriansen party just got here and they don't drink. So they want food." She glanced over her shoulder at the party of four seated next to the wine rack. "I think they're serious eaters," she said in a whisper. "You know, foodies. They asked if we had a seasonal menu. And they're getting a little cross."

"You know what?" Clarissa said. "I can handle this. People like that came into my rest . . . that is, I'm familiar with this type of customer." She smiled. Until she'd smiled, Quill hadn't registered how sad her expression was.

"Sure," Quill said. "I'll just check things out in the kitchen. We have a small staff on Mondays, but there *is* a staff. Kathleen will give you a menu, and we list the evening specials on the blackboard. I'll wait for you in there."

Clarissa nodded and made her way gracefully past the empty tables to the Adriansens and their guests. Something, either the challenge of cooking in an unfamiliar kitchen or the chance to talk to the guests, seemed to have pulled her out of herself. In a matter of moments, she had two women in the party smiling and the men nodding self-importantly.

"Lucky she was here," Dina said. "It could have been a disaster. Not," she added hastily, "that you aren't a good cook, Quill."

"Why *is* she here, Dina?"

"Her cat. She lost her cat. Well, she didn't lose it, exactly; it ran away after M. LeVasque threw it out the back door of the cooking academy. She's put up signs down in the village and they've got that Lost, Stolen, or Strayed thing on the radio . . ."

Quill put her hand up. "Stop. Go back to the reception desk. Call upstairs and see if Doreen needs anything to eat. Jack should be fast asleep by now, but if he isn't, come and get me. Answer the phones. Take messages. Book rooms. Do your job. Stay there until the dining room closes or unless Jack needs me."

"Okay. What if I hear something about Clarissa's cat?"

Quill clapped her hand to her forehead. "The cat. Is it a big orange cat?"

"Clarissa says it's a Maine coon cat. I guess it's huge."

"Okay. I think it's under the hydrangea on the beach. Call Mike. Ask him to get a handful of liver bits from Doreen."

"Doreen has liver bits?"

"Never mind about the liver bits. Ask Mike to get Max's dog cage and ask him to go down to the beach and lure the cat into the carrier. And then Mike can bring it up to the kitchen."

"Clarissa's cat's under the hydrangea bush? I'll tell her right now! She was so worried about that cat."

"Let's see if it's still there. If it isn't, she'll be even more worried. If it is, problem solved. Let's check it out before we get her hopes up."

"Okay." Dina sighed. "I guess this means no movie with Davy, but that's okay. This is pretty much an emergency. I'll let you know if Mike finds the cat."

"Good."

Dina scanned Quill's expression and said wisely, "You want me to go away and get all this rolling."

"Sooner than now," Quill agreed.

Clarissa joined her as she walked into the kitchen.

"Think you can handle this okay?"

Clarissa smiled. "I'd say 'piece of cake' except that good cake's never easy. This will be easy."

"I hope so, for all our sakes. We've got a dishwasher and prep person on hand at the moment. I'll introduce you."

Meg recruited graduate students from the nearby Cornell School of Hotel Administration to handle the basic-skills jobs, and the two nervous kids jumped to attention as Quill and Clarissa came in.

"We heard Meg's in jail!" the girl said.

"It's Devon, isn't it?" Quill said to the tall blond boy holding a pot scrubber. She turned to the slim girl with the tomato sieve. "And you're Mallory. And yes, Meg's in jail, but she's just visiting. Like Monopoly." Quill shut her eyes briefly. Her two universes collided all the time. Mother and manager. "Never mind."

"Kathleen came in looking for a cheese plate with local stuff," Mallory said. "We put together a soft/hard sort of thing, but, Mrs. McHale, there I couldn't find anything other than the ewe's milk cheddar from downstate and some French Brie. I hope that's okay. We couldn't think of anything else to do."

"Things are fine. Meg will be out soon; in the meantime, Chef Sparrow's in charge. Clarissa? This is Devon McAllister and Mallory DiCosta."

"You both did beautifully with the cheese plate," Clarissa said. "Now, I'm going to need both of you to help me get acquainted with this kitchen. Devon? I'll need you to prep a pasta dish, and Mallory, we're going to slap together a nice starter for table thirty-two."

Quill felt herself relax. "And I'll be right outside, if you need me."

Nobody looked up. After a few moments, Quill went out the back door and sat down on the kitchen porch. It was close to eight o'clock and a full moon was rising in the east. The air was cool, and a few clouds drifted across the twilight sky. A satisfying clink of pots and pans sang out from the kitchen. Two stories over her head, Jack was peacefully asleep.

And Myles?

She sighed. She wouldn't think about Myles.

She pulled her sketch pad from one pocket and the stub of a charcoal pencil from the other. She made a quick drawing of the cat under the hydrangea bush and set it aside. Then she checked her cell phone, in case she'd missed a message from Meg. (She hadn't.) There was a brief rustling in the rosemary bush at the front of the garden and Max emerged covered, as usual, with bits of sticks, burrs, and a variety of leaves. He sat down beside her, scratched himself vigorously, and dropped his head in her lap with a contented grunt. Quill combed his coat with her fingers and carefully teased the burrs from his ears. Her cell phone sounded.

"Hey," Meg said.

"Hey, yourself. Are you out?"

"I'm out. Davy's going to drive me back."

"Are you all right?"

Meg snorted. "It'll take a lot more than a couple of hours in stir to crack this cookie."

"Howie couldn't come himself, so he sent his junior associate. I hope it all went smoothly."

"Justin," Meg said. "Justin was great."

Quill was familiar with that note in her sister's voice. "Dina thought we might call

Jerry, in case you needed anything."

"Just cool it, sis."

"Okay," Quill said amiably. "I'll see you in a few minutes, then." She slipped the cell phone back in her pocket and ruffled Max's ears. "Looks like the relationship with Jerry Grimsby is cooling off, Max. I can't say I'm surprised. Two chefs in one household — I'd call that a recipe for disaster." She nudged the sleepy dog. "Ho-ho. I'll tell you the worst thing about Myles being away, Max. No one else gets my jokes."

Max rolled one eye up at her and yawned.

"Actually," Quill said, "that's not the worst thing about Myles being away. The worst thing is sleeping by myself at night. And Myles not seeing the way Jack changes from day to day. Although I do make a quick little drawing of him, every morning, just so Myles can see where he's been and where he's going. That and the photographs."

Somebody pushed the screen door open. Max lifted his head and thumped his tail on the decking. Clarissa came out onto the porch. "Just came out to tell you things are well under control." She smiled down at Max. "That's one of the nicest things about a dog. You can talk to it any time, and it always listens."

"Cats, too," Quill said. She handed the sketch of the cat up to her.

"Bismarck!" Clarissa sat down beside her, and angled the sketch so that she could see it better in the light from the kitchen windows. "Have you seen him? Do you know where he is?"

"He was down by our little beach this afternoon. As soon as Dina told me it might be your cat, I sent our groundskeeper down to bring him back up for you."

"Uh-oh." Clarissa got to her feet. "Bismarck has um . . . issues. Maybe I'd better go give your guy a hand. Oh, shoot. There's the desserts. Table twenty-seven's too drunk to care, but the foursome's going to want berries."

"I can handle the desserts," Quill said bravely. "I'd want to be there, myself, if it were my cat."

"It's not Bismarck I'm worried about," Clarissa said. "Bismarck can take care of himself."

"So can Mike," Quill assured her. The sound of a car coming up the drive made her get to her feet. "And that sounds like Meg. We're saved. She can handle the desserts."

The glare of headlights swept the small parking lot that sat to the left of the gardens.

"She's out already?" Clarissa said. "My gosh. You guys must have fabulous lawyers."

"One way or the other, we're pretty familiar with the criminal justice system," Quill said. "It's more like we're used to the routine."

Clarissa narrowed her eyes at the lights and grabbed her wrist. "Hang on. Do you guys own a Mercedes 450 SL?"

"A what?" Quill squinted into the darkness. The lights on the car dimmed, leaving the parking lot shrouded in moonlight.

"That car." Clarissa's grip tightened. "That long, low-slung shape. Your police force doesn't happen to drive Mercedeses, does it?"

"Good grief. Of course not."

"Then that," Clarissa said grimly, "is not your sister."

She sprang into the kitchen and slammed the door.

5

Soupes! My province *en France* is the home for the best! *Les soupes de poissons* are made with shellfish and fish; *les soupes maigres* are composed with vegetables, you understand. *Les soupes grasse* are prepared with the meat and the bones of the meat. And *les soupes au baton* are based in flour and stirred with a stick. Bravo *les Nicoise* and their *soupes!*

— From *Brilliance in the Kitchen,*
B. LeVasque

A car door slammed and footsteps crunched in the parking lot gravel. Max stood up, his head cocked, his ears tipped forward in mild interest.

Bernard LeVasque walked out of the dark and stepped up onto the porch.

"Where is your manager?" he demanded.

Quill opened her mouth and shut it. She'd never actually met LeVasque, but she had followed in his wake at the open house, as he'd swanned around his fabulous new building. His face was mostly jaw, with little piggy eyes and thinning brown hair. Quill was good at judging ages. LeVasque's boastful bio (the first page in the elaborate and expensive brochure he distributed in every single retail establishment in Hemlock Falls) inferred he was in his mid-forties. She'd be willing to bet her best set of camel-hair brushes he was sixty, at least. He'd had some work done, as Quill's mother used to delicately phrase it. And, despite the presence of his little potbelly, it was pretty clear he worked out at a gym to help hold on to the big age lie.

"I'm Sarah Quilliam-McHale," she said pleasantly. "My sister and I are the owners here."

"The female chef." He sneered. "And you, the female boss."

Quill had been blessed with an equable temperament, so she was a little startled to realize that she was truly pissed off. She unclenched her teeth. "I take it you didn't just drop by to chat?"

"Is Clarissa Sparrow here!?" he demanded.

"Yes, she is. And I must thank you for . . ."

"You have seduced away one of my chefs.

I am here to sue you," he said with relish.

"Down, Max," Quill ordered the dog, who hadn't moved at all except to wag his tail. She grabbed Max by the collar. Max wagged his tail even faster and panted happily. "I don't think I'm going to be able to hold him, M. LeVasque."

LeVasque backed up a few steps. "This dog is vicious?"

"Very," Quill said.

Max wriggled free of her hold on his collar, sat down, and scratched amiably at his neck.

"Max attacks on command," Quill said. "This dog is a Schutzhund."

LeVasque drew his scanty eyebrows together. "The Schutzhund is a breed of Alsatian bred for security work. Very fierce, no? You Americans call it a German shepherd, *peut-être.* That is not a Schutzhund. That is a mutt."

"Appearances can be deceiving, M. LeVasque."

LeVasque spat contemptuously over his left shoulder. "Yes. That is vair-y true, that appearances are deceiving. Mme. Margaret Quilliam looks like a perfectly acceptable *femme.* Instead, she is a thief as well as a *provocateur.* Now there will be a second

78

lawsuit over the steal of my employee's services."

"I have no idea what you're talking about." Quill hoped like anything that Clarissa had made it out of the inn and was back on her way to the culinary academy. "As far as Ms. Sparrow's services are concerned, the whole concept of indentured servitude went out in the eighteenth century. And slavery was declared illegal in 1862. It's a free country and you can't," she concluded, somewhat inelegantly, "sue us for squat."

"No?" He pushed his way past her and marched into the kitchen. Quill, at his heels, was dismayed to see Clarissa chopping raw sugar into a fine powder with a butcher knife.

"Hah! I knew it!" LeVasque put both hands on his hips, jutted out his considerable jaw, and shouted, *"Nom de nom! C'est insupportable!* What are you doing here!"

"I have Monday nights off," Clarissa said coolly. "I can be anywhere I want."

M. LeVasque's eyes were little, beady, and mean. Like Napoleon, he was short. Also rude, aggressive, and militant.

"Sir," Quill said. "I do not want you in my kitchen."

"It's a free country," LeVasque said mockingly. "I can be any-wair I want." He swept

Meg's kitchen with a contemptuous gaze. "And you call this a kitchen? I call this a . . . a . . . midden!"

"Hey!" Quill said. "That's just plain insulting. I really think, M. LeVasque . . ."

"You really think? Hah! Women do not think." He sucked his lower lip, then released it with a popping sound. "I tell you what. You!" He stuck his forefinger under Clarissa's nose. "Are fired. And you!" He swiveled on his feet and waved his fist in the air at Quill. "My lawyers will contact your lawyers!"

Clarissa slapped the butcher knife back in the rack, swept the sugar up in the palm of her hand, and flung it at LeVasque. Then both chefs stood nose to nose and started yelling.

Quill went to the dining room doors and peeked out. Three of the tables were full, as expected, and two of the tables were having such a good time the place could have exploded and no one would have noticed. The anniversary couple, on the other hand, looked scared.

Quill let the doors close, turned around, and put her hands on her hips. She would have to get firm. Clarissa had succumbed to the temptation of the eight-inch sauté pan and advanced on LeVasque with murder in her eye. LeVasque was retreating backward around the prep table. Suddenly, Devon sprang forward, grabbed LeVasque by the collar, and propelled him toward the back door.

The screen door banged. There was a friendly farewell bark from Max the Schutzhund, and LeVasque was gone.

The screen door banged again, and Quill grabbed the eight-inch sauté pan out of Clarissa's hand, in case LeVasque was back. It wasn't LeVasque; it was Mike Santini, the guy who kept the gardens and grounds in such wonderful shape, and Quill had never been so glad to see anyone in all her life. He was small and wiry and tough as an old boot. He'd settle LeVasque's hash in two seconds flat.

"Hey, Mike."

"Hey." He kept a wary eye on the sauté pan in her hand. "I thought Meg was in jail."

"She's out. She should be back any minute." Quill looked dubiously at the pan and hung it back up. Then she sat down in the rocking chair and buried her head in her hands. "Yikes. I can't believe I did that."

"LeVasque has that effect on people," Clarissa said. "I'm sorry."

"You're sorry? You work for that monster. I'm sorry for you!"

"Yeah, well, I don't have a lot of choice, do I?" Clarissa looked at Mike with a smile. "You wouldn't be the Mike that went after my cat, by any chance?"

"That sucker belong to you?" He shook his head admiringly. "Whoo. That's some beauty."

"You have him then?" Clarissa asked. "He didn't hurt you, did he?"

Mike rubbed the back of his neck. "I don't have him, exactly, no."

"Oh, no!"

"I almost had him." He looked at Quill. "I did what you suggested, Boss. I got some of those liver bits of off Doreen and took Max's carrier down to the river. And he was like, half in the bag, so to speak, when you know who shows up."

"You know who?" Quill said, bewildered.

"Carol Ann Spinoza." He rubbed the back of his neck with both hands. "And that cat? That cat don't like Carol Ann Spinoza one little bit. So the cat, like, growls at her and sort of shows his teeth like this." Mike drew his lips back in a horrible grimace. "And Carol Ann Spinoza screams like a banshee. So the cat goes flying off somewheres. But not," he added with satisfaction, "until he, like, bites her a good one on the ankle. So." He shrugged. "I don't have that cat."

Quill clutched at her hair, which was coming down from her top knot again.

"Is this Carol Ann very hurt?" Clarissa asked.

"Nah. She had boots on."

"Boots? Who wears boots in August?"

"Carol Ann," Quill said glumly. "They're part of the uniform. Carol Ann's the animal control officer."

"Thank goodness."

Quill exchanged rueful glances with Mike and said, "Don't thank goodness too soon."

"But that's a good thing, isn't it? I mean, animal control people are experts at catching pets safely."

"She's more likely to shoot it," Mike said. "Or poison it. Or run it over with her animal control Jeep. That Carol Ann's damn mean."

"Shoot Bismarck!" Clarissa said. "She can't do that."

"Not at night, that's for sure," Mike said. "Sheriff's department took away her infrared rifle."

Quill relaxed a little. Clarissa looked even more alarmed.

The screen door banged a third time. Quill was beginning to feel she was in the middle of the second act of *Noises Off.*

Meg came into the kitchen looking so chipper Quill wanted to smack her just on

83

principle. "Hey, guys!" she said. "Is this party just for me?" She spread her arms wide. "Free at last!" She caught sight of Clarissa and cocked her head, just like Max. "Gosh, don't I know you?"

"I'm Clarissa Sparrow."

"From Bonne Goutè. Sure! You're pastry, right? From all I hear, I should take a couple of lessons from you."

Quill stared at her sister in astonishment. Meg had many, many fine character traits, but she was competitive to the bone.

"The secret's in the butter. Irish butter." Clarissa extended her hand and Meg shook it. "I was pinch-hitting in the kitchen while you were . . ." She trailed off.

"In the pokey," Meg said cheerfully. "Quill left a message that the cooking was taken care of. We're lucky you were available."

"Yes. Well, it was a privilege. It was just a fluke I was here. I was out looking for my cat."

"Big orange cat?" Meg said. "There's a big orange cat sitting out in the parking lot."

"Oh, my!" Clarissa said. "Excuse me, will you?" She grabbed her backpack from under the prep sink and took out a collar and leash. On her way out the door, she said, "Those blueberries? They're for table forty-two. I was going to add mascarpone, chopped raw sugar, and a little shortcake. Cake's cooling on top of the Viking."

Meg went to the stove, broke off a piece of the shortcake, and tasted it. Then she looked very thoughtful. "Terrific," she said, absently. "Sensational, in fact. I've only tasted something like this once before."

"Clarissa said it's her standby," Devon offered. "Berries, mascarpone, and a little garnish. All-purpose summer dessert."

"Little lemon, maybe," Meg said. She bent over and inspected the blueberries. "Devon, you can handle this. Add a slice of lemon and some of the fresh mint for garnish. Then plate it and send it out to the dining room."

Devon went obediently to the stove and picked up the pan of shortcake.

Meg looked at the clock over the fireplace. "Shoot. Only eight thirty. I suppose I'd better get back to work."

"Did you have a good time in jail?" Quill asked sarcastically.

"I had an excellent time."

Quill sat up and took a deep breath. "You must be drunk. Or exhausted. I don't care if it is early. We're going to close the kitchen. Mike, please go and tell Kathleen not to seat any walk-ins. And thank you for trying to rescue the cat."

"Anytime," Mike said laconically. "And if there's nothing else except to give that message to Kath, I'll be off home."

"Nothing else." She waited until Mike had disappeared into the dining room and then grabbed her sister's arm. "He came back."

"Who came back?" Meg's eyes widened. "LeVasque came back?"

"Big as life and twice as ugly," Quill said. "He found out Clarissa was here, taking over for you in the kitchen."

"And?"

"And he fired her."

"Golly." Meg ran her hands through her hair, which was short, dark, and tended to stick up like a little kid's if she didn't pay attention. "She's well out of it, is my guess. The guy's a total creep."

Quill winced at yet another slam of the screen door. Operant conditioning, that's what it was called. You were given a negative stimulus over and over until you were ready to scream when it jabbed you again.

"You okay?"

"I keep thinking it's LeVasque."

"It's not. Just me." Clarissa edged her way into the kitchen. Her arms were full of cat. "I brought Bismarck in to say thank you."

There was a lot of Bismarck, and he obscured most of Clarissa's upper torso. He blinked placidly and then, as Max trotted in behind Clarissa, extended a giant paw down to the dog and flexed his claws. Max gave the cat a quick glance and shot through the doors to the dining room.

"Sorry," Clarissa said.

"He's gone up to sleep with Jack," Meg said. "But that's some cat, all right."

"Is Bismarck usually an outdoor cat?" Quill asked. "If so, you might think about keeping him inside for a while. If Carol Ann's on his case, we might have a problem."

"Carol Ann's after that cat?" Meg shook her head. "That woman's a menace. Quill's right. You should think about keeping him inside."

"I usually do."

"Did he slip out the door when no one was looking?" Meg said sympathetically. "How did he get lost in the first place?"

"Bernard," Clarissa said briefly. "I told him I had a cat when he hired me, and he said" — she stuck out her lower lip and adopted a pretty good French accent — "But of course! *Le chat domestique.* What could be more French?' And of course," she continued with some bitterness, "*that* attitude lasted about a week."

"So he threw him outdoors deliberately?"

Meg shook her head. "What an ass."

"Anyway," Quill interrupted. "I'm really glad everything turned out okay and that you got Bismarck back."

"Me, too. Well." Clarissa shifted the cat in her arms. "Thank you for everything. I'd better be off now."

"Off where?" Meg said bluntly.

Clarissa bit her lower lip.

"You guys are all housed at the academy, right? In that annex next to the big building?"

"Yeah. We are."

"And do you really think LeVasque's going to let you back in your apartment?" Meg turned to her sister. "You said LeVasque fired her."

"He sure did," Quill said. "Does he make a habit of it? Or did he mean it?"

"He meant it, all right," Clarissa said. "We've butted heads often enough, but he's one of those people whose word is his bond, if you know what I mean."

"I do," Quill said sympathetically.

Meg pressed on ruthlessly. "So you go back to the annex and what do you think the odds are that all your stuff will be out on the sidewalk?"

"Pretty good," Clarissa said with a laugh. "But he has to let me keep my stuff. In any event, it's my problem, not yours. I can handle it."

Meg folded her arms across her chest. "What about your recipes?"

Clarissa paled.

"Right," Meg said grimly. "What if he gets his slimy little hands on those?"

"They're on my laptop," Clarissa said. "And they're password protected." Her eyes got suspiciously bright. "He wouldn't dare. He wouldn't dare!"

Meg looked at Quill. "Are you thinking what I'm thinking?"

Quill hadn't a clue, but she nodded anyway. What she did know was that Meg didn't trust anybody with the complete list of ingredients to five or six of her most famous dishes. Not even Quill herself. And Meg would stop just short of murder if anyone tried to steal her recipes.

"Tell you what, Clarissa," Meg said. "We'll follow you over to the annex and see that everything's okay. If not, well, we'll take it from there."

Clarissa hesitated.

Meg slung her purse over her shoulder with a purposeful air. "Is that your Ford Escort out in the parking lot? I thought so. We'll take Quill's Honda." She eyed Bismarck, who was staring at her with a sort of benign malevolence. "Tell you what, though. You can take the cat."

6

~Socca~
For six *PERSONNES*

2/3 cup chickpea flour
2 tablespoons LeVasque Extra Virgin Olive
  Oil★
1/2 teaspoon salt
1 cup water

Mix all ingredients and let stand one
hour to allow the flour to absorb all.
Heat oven to 400 degrees. Oil crepe pan,
pour on the pancake mixture, and place
in oven for five minutes. Remove, flip
the pancake, and sprinkle olive oil attractively over the top. Replace pan in
oven for five more minutes. Serve with
salt and pepper.

*LeVasque Extra Virgin Olive Oil is to be
found in fine grocery stores everywhere.
      — From *Brilliance in the Kitchen,*

"You're up to something," Quill said, as she followed Clarissa's battered Escort down the winding drive from the Inn to the village. "You want to clue me in now? Or let me sit here in a state of terror?"

"Terror's good," Meg said. "I don't know that you'll approve, exactly."

"Try me."

"Does Clarissa look at all familiar?"

"I saw her when we took the tour of the academy."

"Anywhere else?"

"Meg, for Pete's sake . . . darn!" Quill braked behind Clarissa at the only red light in town, which was at the intersection of Main and Hemlock Drive. She looked both ways up and down the street. At nine o'clock on a Monday night, there wasn't much happening in Hemlock Falls. All of the wheelbarrows, lawnmowers, ladders, and buckets had been taken in from the sidewalk in front of Nickerson's Hardware. There wasn't much happening at the Croh Bar, either, since those villagers who did eat dinner out ate at six o'clock and went home to catch *American Idol.* The small businesses like Schmidt Realty and Casualty Insurance were closed until morning. The wrought-

iron streetlights illuminated empty side-
walks, and the occasional raccoon foraging
in the white painted planters. Almost all the
buildings on Main Street were made of
stone, which delighted tourists in the day-
time, but gave the place the feel of a cem-
etery at night.

Clarissa gunned through the red light and
took off down the road.

"Worried about the recipes, I think," Meg
said. "Can't say as I blame her."

Quill went through the red light, too.

The Bonne Goutè Culinary Academy lay
past Peterson Park between the Hemlock
Falls Resort and the edge of the village. The
main building was easily accessible from the
road, with a long circular drive. Small,
single-lane roads led off from it at intervals,
much like a European roundabout. The first
lane led out of the parking lot, the second
into the lot, and the third to the annex,
where Bernard LeVasque housed his chefs
and instructors.

The annex was designed with the same
white clapboard, green trim, and exquisitely
polished pine decking as the larger building. Floodlights at the north and south ends
of the roof illuminated the paths and lawns,
without glaring directly into the apartment
windows. The shrubs around the founda-

tion were neatly trimmed and healthy. A large urn spilled white petunias over the front steps. Clarissa slammed to a halt at the portico that sheltered the entrance and killed the lights on the Escort.

"Better park facing the road," Meg said. "Just in case."

"Why do I feel guilty?" Quill said, as she followed Meg's suggestion. "We aren't breaking any laws."

"Not yet," Meg said. "Might be a good idea to turn the headlights off, too."

Quill did that. Then they both sat for a moment. The engine ticked over. Somebody in one of the apartments had the TV on; Quill heard the familiar opening of the ten o'clock news.

Clarissa got out of her car and went inside the annex. Meg poked Quill in the ribs. "You ready?"

"Ready," Quill said firmly. "Why are we whispering?"

"Why not?"

They found Clarissa in the foyer. It was spacious, perhaps twenty by twenty. A row of mailboxes was fixed on the south wall. Quill counted ten. So there must be ten apartments, five to the left and five to the right. Unless there was a laundry room.

Quill pinched herself so that she'd stop

94

obsessing about the layout of the building. A row of brass coat hooks with a shelf underneath for boots took up the wall opposite. The floor was carpeted in the kind of indoor-outdoor carpeting that always smelled funny to Quill; rubbery, with a chemical undertone. The pattern was an inoffensive green, brown, and cream plaid.

Clarissa was taking deep, regular breaths, which, when Quill thought about it, was a less painful way to de-stress yourself than pinching. She'd have to remember that.

"I'm in number eight," Clarissa said. "I didn't get a corner unit. Those go to the chefs with more seniority. It's just down here."

The carpeting kept their movements quiet, for which Quill was grateful.

"Damn!" Clarissa said. "Will you look at what that turkey did!"

Two four-by-four pine boards were nailed across the door to number eight.

"Madame's going to be royally pissed," Clarissa muttered. "He nailed those boards right into the door frame."

"You're locked out of your apartment and you're worried about Mrs. LeVasque being pissed?" Meg said.

Clarissa pried at the boards with her fingers. "It's not even nails. That sucker went and got a drill and put screws in here."

"Crow bar," Quill suggested. "I think there's one in the trunk. From the time Marge and I had to get into what's-his-name's trailer," she said to Meg.

Meg shook her head. "That was before I used it to get into MacAvoy's nudie bar. I didn't put it back."

The door to number seven, which was directly across from Clarissa's, opened up and a sturdy woman of about forty looked out into the hall. She had freckles, brown eyes, and hair that nature had intended to be red. Her hair had received some inexpert assistance in staying that way.

"Clarissa!" she said. "Oh my God. Are you all right?!"

"Hello, Raleigh. Raleigh, this is Quill. And her sister, Margaret Quilliam."

A smile lit her face. "*The* Margaret Quilliam? As in Shrimp Quilliam?"

"And Pork Soup Quilliam," Meg admitted in a self-deprecating way.

Clarissa, Meg, and Raleigh all chuckled, as if at a well-known joke.

"Pork soup?" Quill said. "I've never had your pork soup."

"You never had my pork soup because it's a famous disaster."

"The Shrimp Quilliam, though!" Raleigh

kissed her fingers in Gallic-style appreciation and then seemed to realize they weren't there for a social call. She cast a worried look up and down the hallway. "Why don't you come in? Just for a minute. He said he'd be back. He means to post a guard at the door all night. You don't have much time." She stepped back and let the others into the room.

The apartment was quite pleasant, although the dark-veneered furniture gave it the feel of a hotel. The carpeting was beige, the walls were painted beige, and the curtains drawn over the double doors to the patio were beige, too. A reproduction of the Woodstock poster hung over the three-cushion couch and a ceramic pot of daisies sat on the bookshelf.

"You're Sarah Quilliam," Raleigh said. "The artist?"

Quill nodded. She couldn't think of a famous art disaster to fend off the admiration, so she said awkwardly, "Your rooms are very nice."

"All these places are exactly the same. I haven't had time to put any of my personal stuff in it."

"It looks very comfortable, and that's the main thing."

"It's not very comfortable at the moment," Raleigh said frankly. "Not with the Maitre on the warpath. What in the name of God is going on, Clarissa?"

"I got fired."

"Oh." Raleigh sank down on the couch. "I suppose it was only a matter of time. Wow. Wow." She looked up at them. "What are you going to do?"

"First thing is to get my recipes back." Clarissa crossed her arms, hugging herself, and began to pace up and down the room. "That little creep can't hold on to them. They're my personal property."

"The recipes are intellectual property," Meg said, with the annoying air of someone who knows something you don't. "And they're incredibly valuable. I know someone who can get them back for you but . . ."

"All LeVasque has to do is copy them," Clarissa said. "And then I'm screwed for sure."

Quill poked her sister. "Who do you know that can get them back, Meg?"

"A very good lawyer," Meg said loftily.

"And how do you know recipes are . . . what was the phrase? Intellectual property?"

"As I said. A very good lawyer told me."

"It wouldn't be this Justin Whosis. This associate Howie Murchison's taken on, by any chance."

"It might." Meg flashed her a grin. "And I have a feeling we're going to need a really good . . ."

"Ssst!" Raleigh jumped up from the couch in alarm. "Hear that?"

The building was too solidly built to shake, but there was some sort of thumping and marching around in the hall. Then someone pounded on Raleigh's door.

"Into the bedroom!" Raleigh hissed. "I'll tell him I don't know a thing."

"Not the bedroom," Meg said. "He knows we're here. Our cars are out front. And, excuse me, Clarissa, that car of yours is so ratty that it can't be mistaken for anyone else's. We'll go out that way." She pointed dramatically at the patio doors.

"Raleigh Brewster!*Ouvrez!!*"

"What the hell?" Raleigh muttered.

"He means open up," Quill said.

"Raah-leee?" shrieked a feminine voice.

"And that's Madame," Clarissa said. "She's worse than the Maitre."

Quill slung her purse over her shoulder purposefully. "And I'm with Meg. We should leave. Come on, Clarissa. We'll meet you back at the Inn."

"Ouvrez! Maintenant! Tout de suite!"

"I'll be right there," Raleigh called sweetly. "I just have to get some clothes on! I am totally naked, Madame."

There was a decided pause in the pounding at her door. Quill grabbed Clarissa's elbow and gave Meg a hearty shove toward the patio. Raleigh slid the doors open, and the three of them tumbled out onto the lawn.

"The Inn!" Quill said. "Ten minutes!"

She and Meg made a dead run for the Honda and pulled out of the driveway just as LeVasque fell through the entrance door, tripped up, Quill surmised, by the profusely apologetic Raleigh. A big guy in a nondescript gray uniform made a halfhearted lunge at Clarissa, who neatly evaded him. She tumbled into the Escort. The security guard opened the passenger door, leaned forward, and then leaped back with a shout, nursing his left hand.

"Bismarck strikes again," Quill said. "Ha!"

"Will you step on it, please?" Meg said. "I think that guy has a gun." She pulled out her cell phone. Quill, concentrating on making the turn back onto Main Street at fifty miles an hour, spared her a glance.

"What are you doing?!"

"Hey!" Meg said into the cell. "Dina? Yeah. It's me. No, I'm not mad. No, it's okay. Really. I know how sorry you are. More to the point, I know how foggy you

100

get when you're studying your copepods. Look. You've got to give Davy a call and get him down here right away. Huh? Oh. The culinary academy. The annex. M. LeVasque's in the process of breaking and entering into a private residence. Huh? Just do it. Please. He's doing it right now!" She snapped the cell phone shut and stuck it back in her purse. "Where's Clarissa?"

Quill looked in the rearview mirror. The Escort's headlights were distinctive, mainly because one was dimmer than the other. "Right behind us."

"That jerk isn't after us, is he?"

"Meg! It's dark out there!"

"Well, look for Mercedes headlights!"

"I have no idea what Mercedes headlights look like."

"Put on your turn signal and wave Clarissa over. Where are we?" Meg peered out the window. "Right next to Peterson Park. Pull in next to the kiosk. Right here. Good."

The Escort grumbled to a stop behind them, and Clarissa poked her head out the driver's window. "What's up?"

Quill stuck her head out the window, too. "My question, exactly."

"I created a distraction," Meg said proudly.

The squeal of the Hemlock Falls sheriff's

department cruiser siren made the evening hideous. Quill flinched as the black-and-white flashed by them, red lights whirling. "You certainly did. But why? You aren't . . . oh," she said in a voice of doom. "I see where you're going."

"Well, I don't," Clarissa said.

Quill gave her sister a look she knew to be pitiful. "I can't, Meg. I'm a mother now."

"Pish-tosh," Meg said cheerfully. "She probably has a key, and it's her own apartment and we'll just go in the patio doors, but it won't work if we don't get going *right now.*"

Clarissa sat up so fast she bumped her head on the driver's-side door frame. "Wait. You mean I should go in the back way while the sheriff is out front arresting LeVasque?"

"That's exactly what I mean," Meg said. "But if we don't get on the stick . . ."

"Jump in the back, ladies," Clarissa said. "There's a way through the back fields that will take us right to my back door."

"It's not going to work," Quill said, and she let Meg pull her into the backseat of the Escort. "And I'll end up in jail again, and I will never forgive you, Meg, because if I'm not there when Jack wakes up in the morning, I personally will *pitch a fit the likes which you've never seen!*"

"It'll work," Meg said confidently.

And it did.

"Told you," Meg said smugly, some twenty minutes later. They were seated out on Quill's balcony on the third floor of the Inn. Quill's old rooms looked out on the herb garden. The kitchen was directly below her, if you didn't count the floor in between, and they had a good view of the back parking lot. Clarissa clutched her laptop in one hand, and a glass of red wine in the other.

"Fastest B and E we've ever done, sis. Give me a high five." Meg leaned over the arm of her wicker chair and held her hand up. Quill slapped it with less than enthusiasm. "I swore off this stuff when I had Jack," she said. "And I'm not going to get all tangled up in it again."

"You two make a habit of this?" Clarissa sounded anxious.

"Of course not," Quill said. "But you get all kinds of people coming in and out of a place like ours, and over the years, there've been a few corpses and the two of us got drawn in accidentally. Mostly accidentally," she amended, after turning over their prior cases in her mind.

She sipped her red wine. All through her

pregnancy, and for the eight months while she was breast-feeding, she'd had to give up wine. It wasn't a hardship at all, when you considered the miracle that was her little boy. But it was nice to be able to drink a glass or two with her sister.

"Corpses?" Clarissa said, even more anxiously.

"We didn't commit any of the murders," Meg assured her. "And we've never been convicted of a thing . . . well, Myles would tell you we should have been convicted of meddling, but that's not a crime, it's not even a misdemeanor. So please don't worry. You're perfectly fine."

There was a short silence. And for some reason, it was an uncomfortable one. Quill, a little at sea, looked at her sister, who in turn was looking out at the gardens in a self-satisfied way, and then looked at Clarissa, who seemed miserable and determined, both at once.

"Look!" Clarissa said a little too loudly. "There's something you need to know about me."

"You're not Clarissa Sparrow," Meg said. "You're Clare Robbins, and you've just gotten out of jail for tax fraud."

Quill froze. Then she said, "Oh, dear. Oh my gosh."

"That's my sister," Meg said affection-
ately. "Super speedy with the amazed exple-
tive." She patted Quill on the knee. "That's
one of the reasons she's been so anxious
about our detective activities. You're on
probation, right?"

"Right," Clare said, faintly.

"And parolees get into a lot of trouble if
they associate with known felons. But we
aren't. Known felons, that is. So you can
rest easy."

"Good grief," Quill said.

Clare made a sound that might have been
a laugh. Then she set her glass of wine down
on the little table that sat between the
wicker chairs. "Did LeVasque tell you?"

Meg shook her head. "Nope. It was the
shortcake."

"My shortcake?"

"For the blueberries in that dessert you
made tonight. I stopped in at your restaurant when I was in New York last year."

"Le Tartine," Quill said suddenly. "I
remember. You raved about it, Meg."

"You made the best pastry I've ever had.
And that shortcake tonight . . . well, if your
shortcake's anything to go by, you're the
best baker I've ever met, too. So . . ."

Quill knew what was coming next. She'd
never actually been tied to a set of railroad

tracks with a train coming; at the moment, she felt a lot of sympathy for people who had. But she loved her sister, and if this was a way to get people back into Meg's dining room, she'd support it. Although she'd probably have to keep a closer eye on the accounts and the cash drawer. "You're thinking that she'd be a terrific draw for the kitchen, Meg. And you're right."

"You mean you're offering me a job?"

"Why not? We could use a great pastry chef."

Clare set her wineglass down next to Quill's and started to cry.

"I'd like to try it out for a month or so," Meg said. "What do you think?"

"You don't know what I've done," Clare said. "Hang on a minute, will you?" She put her hands over her eyes, went very still, and counted backward from ten. She sighed heavily, sat up straight, and wiped her eyes with the bottom of her T-shirt. "Okay. It's under control. I've just been on edge for so long, and you've been so great about this, Meg, that I kind of lost it."

Quill began to get out of her chair. "I'll get a tissue."

"No, no. Sit back. I'm okay now. Thanks. And I want to tell you what happened. I didn't get to spend a whole lot of time in your kitchen, Meg, but it was long enough to see that you guys are really tight together. You know what I mean? You all seem to take care of each other. Look at the way you handled the thing with Dina, Quill. And your waitstaff loves you. And those kids in the kitchen think you walk on water. Anyway." She took another deep breath. "I couldn't take a job with you all if you weren't able to trust and like me in the same way. So.

"This is what happened.

"I met Paul in Paris. We were both students at the CB."

"Cordon Bleu," Meg said.

Quill scowled. "I know that."

"Yes. Well. Paul had just gotten his CPA."

"That's certified public accountant, Meg."

"I know that, Quill."

"Wasn't sure. Sorry, Clare. I'm still a little ticked about Meg's trip to jail." The two of them also had decided, without a word, that the atmosphere needed lightening. Clare's tears were still very near the surface.

"Paul wasn't thrilled at the idea of spending his life totaling up numbers for other people. So we decided to come back home to New York and open a restaurant. He'd handle the entrees. I'd specialize in the pastries."

"Your pastries are brilliant," Meg said. "You should have seen the reviews in *Gourmet* and *L'Aperitif,* Quill."

"Thanks. I worked hard at them. Well. Paul took over raising the money. He's a Harvard business school grad, so he hit up a bunch of his loaded buddies for the cash for the start-up. It was a lot," she said soberly. "A couple of million. I found the space. We took over a restaurant that had gone belly-up. I found this wonderful architect who remodeled the whole place, and we opened La Tartine two springs ago.

"I don't know when we began to run into trouble. Business was great. We were lucky with our reviews and at one point, we were booked four months in advance. Then . . ." Clarissa stopped and struggled for composure. "Then we hired a maitresse d'. A friend of Paul's from his accounting days, and they took off. For the Seychelles, it turned out. No extradition.

"I started handling the finances myself, of course. And I found nothing had been paid. Not the architect, not the builder, no one. Just the food suppliers and the wine guys."

All three of them knew how alert food suppliers were to defaulting restaurants. It was pay on delivery or no delivery.

"Then the investors started calling. And I

couldn't find the money."

"In the Seychelles, was it?" Meg asked. "The rat."

"It was worse than that. I'm still not exactly sure how he did it — I just blanked out when the lawyer tried to explain it to me, and to tell you the truth, I don't think he quite got it himself."

"Public defender?" Quill said.

"Just some very nice guy from Albany Law School. He tried his best. Anyhow, it looked as if I'd helped steal it. Paul had gotten my signature on a bunch of transfers. I never looked at . . ." Clare stopped again. "Anyhow. It was in all the papers. You know what happened. I was sentenced to jail for fraud for two years. I got out early on parole. Mainly because Bernard LeVasque vouched for me and guaranteed me a job. But it was a job with a contract. I can't quit. I mean, I can, but there's this huge financial penalty if I do. And if I'm fired . . . there's a good chance my parole will be revoked."

She folded her hands in her lap. "So that's it. You still want to hire me?"

"Not to do the accounts of course," Meg said. "But we're awfully glad to have you." She patted Clare's back. "You're going to love it here."

7

∼SALADE NICOISE∼
FOR FOUR *PERSONNES*

4 ripe Roma tomatoes
1 thinly sliced peeled cucumber
1 head red-leaf lettuce
1/2 cup young lima beans
4 marinated artichoke hearts with stems
1 bulb of fennel, peeled and sliced thin
1 small Vidalia onion, chopped
2 hard-boiled eggs, attractively sliced
8-ounce can of tuna filet in water
16 Kalamata olives
4 seasoned toasted croutons*
1/2 cup olive oil
1/4 cup red wine vinegar
Handful chopped basil
1 large garlic clove, peeled and crushed

Divide first ten ingredients in four por-
tions and arrange in a beautiful style on
a large plate. Mix last four ingredients

with a wire whisk, and divide among the plate. Add toasted croutons.

*Recipe may be downloaded from my website.

— From *Brilliance in the Kitchen,*
B. LeVasque

Jack banged his spoon into the middle of his bowl of granola, hopped off his booster chair, and took a running leap onto the foot of Quill's bed. Max barked and jumped up to join him. Quill slid her charcoal pencil into the nightstand drawer and turned her sketch pad face out.

"Who's this?" she asked in the voice she used just for Jack.

"Me," Jack said. Then, with simple immodesty, "I'm gorgeous."

"And who told you that?"

"Gram!" Jack shouted. Then one fist full of Max's ear, he demanded, "Where is she?"

"Out for a walk."

"Without me?"

"Yes."

"Why?"

"Because mornings are our time, Jack."

"Why?"

"Because I love you," Quill said.

"Why?"

When she was pregnant with Jack, Quill had abandoned her business management classes at nearby Cornell University (to the silent but heartfelt relief of her employees) for classes in Child Development, Know Your Toddler, and Excellent Parenting. The teacher in Know Your Toddler had been very clear about the pitfalls during Terrible Twos. The "why?" Quill gathered, was like the zucchini plants in the vegetable garden: endlessly productive of yet more "whys."

A familiar rat-a-tat sounded at her door. "Do you hear that knock at the door?"

Jack cocked his head. "Yes."

"Whose knock is that?"

"Auntie Meg!"

"Would you tell her to come in, please?"

"All by myself?"

"Yes."

"Then, no. I will not." His smile was seraphic.

"Okay. I will." Quill threw the duvet aside and started to get out of bed.

Jack shook his head. "No. No. No. This is my job."

The door opened, and Meg poked her head inside the room. "You guys up already?"

"She did it herself, Mommy," Jack said. "Ha-ha!"

Meg bent, scooped him up, and gave him a kiss. "Hey, pumpkin face."

"Hey, cereal face," Jack said. "Hey, dog face. Hey, Meg face."

"Jeez." Meg dumped him next to Max, then perched on the bed herself. "The kid's turning into a terror." She tickled his tummy. "A terror."

What with the dog, her sister, her son, and herself, Quill figured it was a good thing she had a queen-sized bed. She drew her knees up to her chin to give everyone more room and said, "Have you been down to the kitchen yet?"

"Tuesday's my day off."

Quill waited expectantly.

"Of course I've been down to the kitchen. She's doing fine. She was up at four to set the bread rising, which was very cool. And she didn't say a thing about getting a brick oven, although we've got to think about that, Quill, if we're going to get serious about breads."

"Okay." They were having a good year, for once, despite the low attendance in the restaurant. Of course, it helped a great deal that Myles's earnings meant she didn't have to worry about her own draw. "I'll run it by John when we do the quarterly accounts. If she's still here."

"I hope this works out. She sure has an awful story. That ex-husband sounds like a total jerk. Lied to her, stole money, forged her signature, cheated the government, set her up for the fall, and then ran off to the Seychelles with the hostess. Yuck!"

"Yuck doesn't even begin to cover it."

"What this country needs," Meg said, "is tort reform."

"Hah?" Quill said.

"Here's this poor woman, no money, no friends, just a lot of pissed-off creditors, and what does she get? Some overworked schmuck from the public defender's office who doesn't know a general ledger from General Motors. If she'd had better representation, she wouldn't have served those eighteen months in the slam."

"Meg, I don't think tort reform has anything to do with criminal acts."

"No?" Meg said in a superior way.

"No."

"I suppose I could find out," Meg said reflectively. "Justin would know."

"I can see that you're dying to."

"What do you mean by that?"

"I see that the very capable Justin Whosis is about to get a phone call from my sister."

"Martinez. Justin Martinez. And he's more than just capable. He's gorgeous."

"Wow," Quill said, startled at the vehemence in her sister's voice. "He must be. Are you going to bring him by for dinner?"

"Maybe. We'll see."

"And Jerry?"

Meg picked up Jack's hands and started a game of patty-cake.

"Okay. We have a 'no comment, Your Honor' in regard to Jerry Grimsby. While we're on legal subjects, so to speak, what's the status of this alleged assault you committed? You've what? Been released on your own recognizance? Is that the right expression?"

Jack snatched his hands away and began to hum tunelessly to himself. Meg leaned back against Quill's knees. "That's the right expression. Next step is a hearing, and Justin says once Howie gets to meet LeVasque up close and personal, the court will give me a medal instead of a sentence. LeVasque was," Meg said with sudden intensity, "absolutely foul. Dina saw it all, and she's incapable of saying anything but the absolute truth, so I'm not worried one little bit. Besides," she added, in a more practical tone, "Justin thinks we should meet with LeVasque and his lawyers and work something out so that the civil complaint is dropped. Justin says if the civil complaint is dropped, the criminal charges should go away, too. Justin says so, anyway."

Quill wondered if she was going to get very tired of the phrase "Justin says."

"Mommy!" Jack said. "There's a rat-a-tat-tat at the door!"

"And whose knock would that be?" Quill said.

"Gram!"

"Would you tell her to come in, please?"

Jack tilted his head to one side while he considered his options. The first was appealing: No. No. No. But then Mommy would tell Gram to come in, and Jack would have missed his chance, or worse yet, Gram would come in all by herself, so he shouted, *"Come in, Gram!"* and Doreen walked in the door.

"Hey, Doreen," Meg said.

"Morning, Meg. Morning, Quill. Morning, young Jack-a-rooty. You got your walkin' shoes on?"

"No," Jack said, who in fact did have his shoes on. "I put them on Max."

Doreen hefted Jack onto one hip. "We got a playdate at the park," she said. "See you later. And, Quill? That big old orange cat's tramping around downstairs and that Miz Fredericks's takin' on something fierce. And Dina said don't forget you got that talk."

Quill stared at her. "Talk?"

"To them WARP people. About running a bed-and-breakfast?"

Quill flopped back against the pillows and pulled the duvet over her head. "Oh, shoot! I forgot!"

"I don't know what you know about running a bed-and-breakfast, anyway," Doreen said. "This is an inn. We've got twenty-seven rooms . . ."

"I know that, Doreen."

"And a full restaurant. We even" — Doreen took a breath — "have a gol-durned beach. This bed-and-breakfast stuff is for amateurs."

"True," Quill said. "Dang." She felt her forehead. "I may be coming down with something."

"Well, I sure as heck hope not," Doreen scolded, "because if you got it, Jack's gonna get it. And if you are sickening for something, it'd better wait until noon, because your talk is at ten with coffee and time for Q and A."

"I was just sort of guessing about being sick," Quill said meekly. "I feel fine, really. Tell Dina I'll be there as soon as I get dressed. Ask Clare to put Bismarck in the garden shed or something, will you?"

"That the skinny brunette in the kitchen?

Thought her name was Clarissa."

"She's Clare," Meg said. "And she can put Bismarck in the pantry."

"Got it."

Quill shoved Max onto the floor and waved them all out. "Whatever. Bye-bye, Jack."

"Come with us, Max! Bye-bye, Mommy! Bye-bye, Auntie Meg. Bye-bye, room! Bye-bye, rug. *Bye, bye, bye!*" Jack's shouts trailed him down the hall and finally died away.

"How to run a bed-and-breakfast?" Meg said. "You've got to be kidding me. You're much better qualified to give a talk on how to raise a toddler without going totally insane."

Quill sighed. "They asked and I said yes, in a weak moment." She looked at her watch. "But it's not until ten, and it's only nine, now. I'll think of something. But first, I've got to get Clare onto the payroll. I'm listing her as a temp until we see how this works out. Which reminds me, is she Robbins or Sparrow?"

Meg shrugged. "Sparrow's her maiden name. The divorce isn't final yet, so legally she's still Robbins but if I'd been married to that fathead, I'd go back to my maiden name so fast you couldn't see me for spit." Suddenly, she jumped off the bed. "The day's a-wasting! I'm gone! Call me if you need me."

The door shut behind her before Quill could ask her (a) if she was going to give Jerry the standard "it's not you, it's me" farewell speech or (b) if she was planning on hedging her bets and dating both guys at once. Then she figured it wasn't her business anyway, but going downstairs to smooth Muriel Fredericks's ruffled feathers was, so she got up and went into the kitchen to get dressed.

In the old days, before she'd married Myles, her rooms at the Inn had consisted of a bedroom, a small kitchen, and a living room, and she'd loved them. It was quiet, up on the third floor, and she'd used low-keyed neutral colors throughout. It'd been her refuge against the long days handling the usual furors at the Inn. And she'd had plenty of closets.

When she'd married Myles, she'd moved to his cobblestone house and her old rooms became a suite, much in demand by those guests who stayed for more than a long weekend. And she still had plenty of closets.

Jack's arrival, and her return to the Inn while Myles was away on assignment, had demanded yet another set of changes. Mike had installed a window in her large walk-in closet and turned it into a bedroom for Jack. When Doreen was widowed, Mike had built a connecting door to the adjacent room, and Doreen rented out her house in town and moved herself in. The only real problem with this arrangement was that there weren't any closets.

So Quill kept her clothes stashed in a variety of places. Underwear, nightgowns, and other lingerie went into the oak chest she used as a coffee table. Shoes, jeans, T-shirts, and shorts went into the cupboards over the tiny stove. And her skirts and silk tees hung in the broom closet.

Quill didn't have time to decide what to wear every morning, so she kept it simple. Three calf-length cotton skirts and six silk tees in the summer, and three fine wool skirts and six silk sweaters for the winter. All of her clothes were in shades of bronze, amber, peach, and celadon. (Dressing in black made her feel like Mrs. Danvers in the old Gothic horror story *Rebecca.* Dressing in white was a stain waiting to happen.) So she kept to colors that suited her red hair and hazel eyes and only occasionally yearned for more choices.

She took a fast shower, dressed, and came down the big staircase to the foyer to find Dina pink-faced and exasperated behind the mahogany reception desk.

"*There* you are," Dina said fiercely. "Quill, I know what you've said about not beating up the guests but I am like, up to here with that Fredericks person!"

"Oh, dear."

"That woman," Dina said darkly, "is allergic to everything. Plants, animals, carpets . . ."

"Some people are very allergic, Dina. We have to be sympathetic."

". . . Cloth, fur, wood, smells . . . Let me just ask you one tiny thing, Quill. Just one tiny thing."

Quill waited a bit, then when nothing more was forthcoming said, "And the one tiny thing is what?"

Dina leaned forward and dropped her voice to a fierce whisper. "Have you ever seen her actually *sneeze!?*"

Quill thought back. "No. Come to think of it, I haven't."

Dina leaned back in her chair and tossed her pencil onto the desktop with a satisfied expression. "There you are. Just a BFW."

This was Inn-speak for Big Flipping Whiner.

"Hmm. Where is she?"

"She's in the Tavern Lounge, with the rest of them," Dina said glumly. "A big FedEx package came for one of them this morning, and they all lit out together with it. Wait a minute. You have a couple of messages." She picked up the pink stack of While You Were Out slips and handed them over.

Quill paged through them one by one: the Golden Pillars Travel Agency wanted to book a party of fourteen at Christmastime. That was good. The rest of the calls were from villagers: Harvey Bozzel, Hemlock Falls's best (and only) advertising executive; Nadine Peterson, owner and chief hairdresser at Hemlock Hall of Beauty; the Reverend Mr. Shuttleworth. Quill looked up in bewilderment. "Most of these are from the Chamber of Commerce members."

"They sure are," Dina said fervently.

Quill waited a moment, and then said, "Do you know what it's about?"

"Is it gossiping to tell you that everyone's in a huge flap over the Welcome Dinner?" Dina adjusted her red-rimmed spectacles with her forefinger. "I know how you feel about gossiping. It's number whatever on your Innkeeper's Rules List."

"I'm looking at my watch," Quill said, doing just that. "And the reason I'm looking at my watch is that it's 9:45 in the morning and you hadn't started to drive me bananas yet. I was starting to get worried."

"So it's not gossiping." Quill's expression must have reflected her feelings — well beyond exasperation at the moment and verging into annoyance — because Dina flung both her hands up and said, "It's because I'm so contrite over blowing Meg in to the cops. I'm trying to do everything exactly by the book."

"Why is there a flap over the Welcome Dinner?" Quill smacked herself in the forehead with the palm of her hand. "Oh my gosh. Everyone wants an invitation."

"It would seem so."

"And there's only what . . . thirty spaces?"

"That's about it."

"And twenty-four Chamber members, which doesn't account for the spouses and significant others."

"Bingo."

"And the mayor's using town funds to pay for it, so everybody . . ." Quill stopped herself. "Why is everyone calling me?"

Dina took the pink slips out of her hand, flipped through to the bottom one, and gave it back to Quill.

Congratulations! I have asked the mayor to appoint you host for the Welcome Dinner! You are now in charge of the guest list. Warm regards, B. LeVasque.

"He told me to write it down exactly as

he said," Dina said. "And I stuck *faithfully* to rule number three, which is never insult a member of the public."

Quill crumpled the paper in her fist. "That little *twerp!*"

"Harassment," Dina said. "Clarissa said the man's a master at it. And you know what else he said, just before he hung up on me? 'Tell her that's just the beginning.' "

"He did, did he?"

The Inn phone sounded its gentle chimes. Dina picked it up and said, "Good morning. This is the Inn at Hemlock Falls. How may I . . . oh, hi, Mrs. Doncaster. Quill? The Welcome Dinner?"

Quill shook her head vehemently, like Jack: No! No!

Dina rolled her eyes and shrugged. "She's not available at the moment, but I'll get her the message as soon as I can. Yes. No. No, ma'am, I have no idea what her cell phone number is. I'll tell her, you bet. Good-bye." She replaced the phone in the cradle.

Quill leaned over the desk. "If you give out my cell phone number to anyone from the Chamber, I will be really, really mad."

"Right."

"And you have no idea where I am today. Got it?"

"Got it. What are you going to do?"

Quill sighed. "After I murder Bernard LeVasque or before? Before I murder Mr. LeVasque, I want you to put every single Chamber member's name in a hat — and anyone else who calls about tickets, for that matter — and then I want you to pull thirty names out at random and make a list. That's who'll be on the list for the Welcome Dinner. And when people call about it, you tell them we made the list up by random selection and that the list will be up in the post office this afternoon."

"Wow," Dina said. "I thought maybe you'd be, like, lost without those management courses at Cornell, but this is really good. Very executive."

"Thank you," Quill said. "It comes from being a mother, I think. And now I am going to run and hide in the Tavern Lounge."

Quill walked down the short hallway to the Tavern Lounge.

The Inn had started as a trapper's rest stop back in the late seventeenth century. The trapper's shack, owned by a lady of dubious reputation, was no more than twenty feet by twenty feet, and Quill had some compunction about the stone on the foundation engraved: EST 1668. But the original stone footers were, in fact, directly under the reception desk. In the two hundred and fifty years since the demise of the fur trade, the building had sprawled, becoming in turn, a farmhouse, a gentleman's residence, an academy for wayward girls, and just after the Civil War, an actual wayside Inn with fourteen rooms and an outhouse.

The Tavern Lounge had been added on sometime in the late 1920s, when village burghers had set it up as a speakeasy. The floors were flagstone, and the long, splendidly polished mahogany bar was the pride of Quill's modest brochure. French doors led out to the stone terrace, and the view of the falls was framed by Mike's meticulous landscaping.

The room was comfortably furnished with round tables and deeply cushioned chairs. The cobblestone fireplace at the north end was filled with late August roses and sprays of lavender well past its prime. The lounge didn't officially open until noon, when it was legal to serve liquor, but the members of WARP found it a convenient place to gather, when they weren't off touring the countryside in their rented stretch limos.

The members of WARP had pushed two of the round tables together and sat in satisfied proximity to one another, wearing identical T-shirts. William Knight Collier glanced at his watch and said cheerfully, "Right on time."

William Knight Collier was always cheerful. Quill thought he must have been one of the few mortgage bankers to survive the notorious crash of 2008. Or maybe he hadn't, and the resulting financial catastrophe had driven him mad.

"Like 'em?" Big Buck Vanderhausen swept his meaty hand over his torso. "Got 'em delivered this morning."

The T-shirts weren't exactly matching, Quill realized. They were all made of the same material, a navy blue knit that looked quite expensive. But the slogans across the chests were all different. Big Buck's read: *A Penny Saved Is a Penny Earned.* Valerie Barbarossa's said: *Don't Spend It All at Once.* Anson Fredericks's skinny chest trumpeted, *Look After Your Pennies and the Pounds Will Take Care of Themselves.* The only shirt at odds with all this clichéd advice was Collier's, which was emblazoned, *Penny-Wise, Pound-Foolish.*

"Mr. Collier is our contrarian," Valerie said. "And Mrs. Fredericks just stepped outside to make a phone call, so you can't see her T-shirt, but it says, *Save for a Rainy Day.*" Her eyes twinkled. "You just look as if you might be interested. Please, sit down.

We're really anxious to hear what you can tell us about running a bed-and-breakfast." She glanced over at Anson. "I don't think we need to wait for Muriel, do you, Anson? Mrs. McHale has been good enough to start on time, and I think we should be just as courteous."

"No problem," Anson said. "Go ahead, Quill."

Quill glanced at the clock over the bar. It was just on ten. "I'll be happy to tell you what I know." She drew a chair out and sat down facing them. "I know that you all value your privacy, and I don't want to intrude. But what's your interest in a bed-and-breakfast? As a place to visit, as a group? Or," she hazarded, "as part of your investment club?"

"Investment club," Valerie mused. She tapped her lips reflectively. She was the type of grandmotherly lady Quill didn't see much of anymore. Most of the older women who came to the Inn paid a lot of attention to their hair, and their jawlines, and dressed in trendy jeans and chunky jewelry. They usually started the day with a jog. (Meg called them Mrs. Fletchers.) Mrs. Barbarossa was happily round, with snow-white hair and small, wire-rimmed glasses over her bright blue eyes. She was very fond of rhinestone brooches, which she pinned on the lapels of her print dresses. This morning's was especially awash with color, glittering blue stones surrounded by large fake pearls. She'd placed it just above the *Don't* on her T-shirt. "I suppose we are, in a way."

"The reason I'm asking is that I'd like to tell you what you want to know about running a small inn, rather than what you don't. Because," Quill said, happily settling into the topic, "that's really what a bed-and-breakfast is all about. Running a small, exquisite inn."

"Any money in it?" Big Buck asked. He was the only one of the group that looked really at home in a T-shirt. It stretched tightly over his considerable belly, and he wore a leather vest.

"Not a fortune, by any means. But it can be a lot of fun for active retirees, for example. It helps a lot if you have another source of income."

For some reason, a wave of merriment swept the table.

"I'd like to know how much it would cost to hire somebody like Bernard LeVasque to run the kitchen," Collier said. He brushed at invisible lint on his sleeve with a finicky flick of his fingers.

"Really?" Quill raised her eyebrows.

"Good heavens. Well, I can't think of a B and B operation that would cover the costs of a chef of his reputation."

"We asked him to create a brunch for us this morning," Mrs. Barbarossa confided. "And it was absolutely splendid."

"You did?" Quill said. "That's amaz— well, I mean . . ." She floundered for a second. "If you look at the costs involved with that, I'm sure you can see that having him around full time would involve . . . considerable expense."

"Hmmm," Collier said. "I see your point."

Quill bit her lip. She would not, she absolutely would not stoop to asking how much the obnoxious little toad had charged these poor people. "Umm . . ." she began diffidently. "If you don't mind my asking . . ."

"Anson!" Muriel flung open the French doors from the terrace with a crash and covered the distance to the table in three huge leaps. She caught sight of Quill, shrieked in a polite way, and covered her mouth with her palm. *"Swine flu!"* she shouted through her palm. "This place is infested with swine flu!"

"Don't be absurd," Mrs. Barbarossa snapped. "What in the world are you talking about?"

Muriel's washed-out blue eyes fixed on Quill with surprise. "You don't look sick."

"I'm not sick," Quill said tartly. "I'm perfectly fine."

Muriel pinched her nose shut, but she sat down (at some distance from Quill). "We went to Bonne Goutè this morning for a perfectly lovely breakfast and M. LeVasque was kind enough to let me know that there was . . . some kind of illness here."

"He did, did he?" Quill said grimly.

"He was a perfect gentleman about it, I must say. But it worked on me, you know? And when the driver was bringing us back here, I was thinking about it and thinking about it, so I called M. LeVasque back."

"And he told you we had swine flu?" Quill realized she was on her feet with her fists clenched. Muriel scooted her chair back a few feet.

"Not exactly. I called the cooking academy on my cell and left a message. I begged him, *begged* him to tell me what he knew, and I just now got the call back."

"What did he say?" Quill's voice was deceptively mild.

Her eyes rolled dramatically in her husband's direction. "We have to all check out of here right now!"

"Which is what M. LeVasque wants,"

Quill said calmly. "Everyone in this inn is perfectly well, perfectly healthy, and absolutely fine. M. LeVasque is annoyed with me because one of his best chefs has decided to work in our kitchens instead of for that . . . that . . ." Quill bit her lip, aware that she was about to growl. "Anyway. This is a dirty business tactic, and I'm not going to stand for it." She nodded to them. "Do you mind if we have our talk at another time? Perhaps this afternoon? We can give you a wonderful cream tea here in the lounge about four o'clock."

"Why, thank you!" Mrs. Barbarossa said. "May I ask where you're going now?"

"I'm going to find LeVasque and knock his block off."

8

In the best kitchens, a calm temperament is all to the good.
> — From *Brilliance in the Kitchen,*
> B. LeVasque

Quill was so mad she swept through the dining room without checking to see how the diners were getting on. She straight-armed the swinging doors and stamped into the kitchen, only vaguely aware that Dina was trotting along behind her, trying to get her attention.

"Not now, Dina." She nodded briefly to Clare, who was staring past her with a bemused expression, and raised her hand in greeting at Elizabeth Chou, whose mouth was open in alarm.

Elizabeth was an exceptionally taciturn person. Quill came to a halt and demanded, "What!?"

Clare pointed. Quill turned around. Dina

was hanging on to a guy in a brown uniform who was courteously trying to shake her off. He had a pleasant face, thinning brown hair, and was probably in his early forties. Quill had never seen him before in her life. She didn't recognize the uniform, either.

Dina let go of his arm, and he raised his hand in a sort of salute. "Officer Dooley Banks, ma'am. Department of Environmental Conservation. Are you Sarah Q. McHale?"

Officer Banks delivered this inquiry in the same tone of voice that state troopers ask for a driver's license. For one cowardly moment, Quill thought about denying that she was, in fact, Sarah Q. McHale, but she said, "Yes, sir."

"I'm investigating a report of an illegal beach."

"An illegal beach," Quill said, as if repeating the phrase would make it more comprehensible. "Yes. I see."

"I've been down to inspect the area in question, ma'am, and I have to ask you for the permits."

Quill nodded. "The permits." Then, "Wait! Are you talking about our beach?"

"Yes, ma'am."

"The one Mike and I put in by the river?"

"Yes, ma'am."

"A permit?" Quill said, with a sinking feeling. "We need a permit?"

"Yes, ma'am." He hitched his belt up. "There is a substantial fine attached to interference with a navigable waterway." He paused. "Ten thousand dollars a day, I'm afraid."

"Ten thous . . ." Quill swallowed hard.

"We take our environmental concerns seriously in New York state, ma'am."

"Well, of course you do," Quill said.

"The only way you can navigate the Hemlock River is in an inner tube," Clare said tartly. "This is ridiculous, officer."

"I went down it in a kayak, once," Elizabeth offered.

"And it'll handle a canoe," Dina said.

"There you are," Officer Banks said. "Navigable."

Quill put her hands on her hips. "Everybody please be quiet. Right now."

An obedient silence filled the room.

"I'll be happy to obtain a permit," Quill said. "I'm truly sorry that I didn't get a permit in the first place. If you can tell me where to go to get one, I'll do it right now."

"That'd be our Syracuse office. In the meantime, if I could take a look at the engineering report, Mrs. McHale?"

"The engineering report?"

"Yes. Regulations require . . ."

Quill held her hand up and laughed hollowly. "We filed that with our . . . um . . . engineer."

"Maybe he could fax it over," Dina said helpfully.

Quill glared at her.

Dina smiled and beamed flirtatiously at the conservation officer. "You are aware, of course, of the Hemlock Falls riverfront project."

"Can't say as I am, ma'am."

Dina frowned. "I can't say I'm surprised. Annoyed on your behalf, of course. They never seem to keep the guys in the front line appraised of *anything.*"

"You can say that again," Officer Banks said.

"Of course, a guy like you must have heard rumors, at least."

"Some," Officer Banks admitted. He ran his finger around his shirt collar in an uneasy way.

"But you're not allowed to talk about it, either. Well! All I can say is my graduate class in river morphology took an interest in the beach project and did a pilot study like you wouldn't believe. My professor sent the whole thing on to the Secretary in D.C. to use as a template for further studies in

136

similar situations."

"The Secretary," Officer Banks said, with an inflection that gave it a capital letter, just like Dina.

"The very same. You should be getting a memo about the changes in the regs any day now, as a matter of fact. My professor has worked with — you know — the Secretary — on other projects, and do you know what?" Dina stood on tiptoe and brought her face close to his. "I think this study may change the way we handle navigable riverfront projects *completely.*"

"Wow." Officer Banks shook his head.

"So, sure, we can get a copy of the study to you. But they'll have to black out quite a bit."

"Pilot study, huh?"

"Yes, sir."

Officer Banks grinned. "Okay. Pilot study it is." He put his hat back on his head and carefully adjusted the brim. "Mrs. Mc-Hale?"

"Yes, officer," Quill said. Her voice sounded faint to her own ears, so she said "A-hum!" in a very authoritative way.

"This pilot study's complete?"

"Oh, yes. Absolutely."

"Then what we recommend at the home office is that these pilot studies be dismantled sooner than quick."

"Yes, sir."

"I'll be off now, ma'am."

"Thank you, sir."

He touched one finger to the brim of his hat and walked out the back door.

"Ten thousand dollars a day." Quill sat down in the rocking chair by the fireplace and put her head between her knees.

"Dina, I am in *awe,*" Elizabeth Chou said. She raised her hand, palm up, and she and Dina exchanged a complicated series of slaps. "Was that smart, or what?"

"It was smart," Quill said. "It was brilliant. But now we have to dismantle my beautiful beach."

"I'll get Mike on it," Dina said. "Although we could go ahead and get the permits. If you want, I can get a couple of guys from the grad school in to do an engineering report for you. The whole thing will take a while, but I bet you anything by next year we can have the beach back again."

"That would be wonderful. I mean, not only has it been a real draw for us, but it's one in the eye for that fat little Frenchman."

"You mean LeVasque?" Clare asked.

"Who else?" Quill jumped out of the chair and began to pace around the kitchen. "Spreading rumors about swine flu. Having

Meg arrested. And now this! Turning us in to the DEC, for Pete's sake! That little weasel thinks he can harass me out of business, does he? Well, he's got another think coming."

"This is all my fault," Clare muttered. "I'm so sorry."

"It isn't your fault at all," Quill said warmly. "He and Meg had locked horns long before you came to work for us. Well, a couple of hours, anyhow. What I can't figure out is why? What did we ever do to him?"

"He doesn't need a reason," Elizabeth said. She adjusted her chef's hat on her sleek black hair with a defiant hand. "He's just a vindictive creep."

"But why now?" Quill said. "The academy's been up and operating successfully for several months. Goodness knows he could have come by long before this. We aren't taking any business away from him. He's taking business away from us."

"Who knows what evil lurks in the heart of men?" Dina said. "I'm going to go put all those names for the Welcome Dinner in a hat, now, Quill."

"Good. And you'll talk to Mike about our beach?"

"I'm right on it." She pushed open the door to the dining room and then let it swing shut. "Uh-oh."

"Uh-oh?" Quill walked up behind her, opened the door a crack, and peered out. Then she let fly a word she almost never used and pulled Dina backward.

"What is it?" Clare asked, alarmed. "Is the DEC guy back?"

"I wish," Dina said. "It's Carol Ann. Quick! Everybody out the back!"

"Too late," Quill said, as the doors swung wide.

"So here's where you all are." Carol Ann Spinoza marched in, chin thrust out and with a militant glitter in her eye. "You've been ducking me all morning." As always, she was surrounded by the aroma of fabric softener and soap.

"Can't imagine why," Dina muttered.

Carol Ann swiveled slowly, like the turret guns on the top of a tank. "You talking to me, Dina?" she asked sweetly.

The office of Hemlock Falls Animal Control did not require its officers to wear a uniform, which hadn't fazed Carol Ann a bit. She wore starched black jeans, thigh-high motorcycle boots, and a perfectly ironed black T-shirt with *Hemlock Falls Animal Control Officer* in large white letters on the front.

Despite the ominous outfit, Carol Ann at

first glance looked like the winning candidate for the Strawberry Queen contest held every year in July. Her bouncy blond hair was drawn up into a billed hat lettered *HFACO*. Her bright white teeth flashed in a sticky-sweet smirk. Her peachy complexion was free of any sort of blemish (other than a deceptively kind expression). She chimed when she walked, primarily due to the equipment hanging from her narrow waist. A brown leather belt punched with grommets held a pair of handcuffs (for belligerent pet owners), a choke chain, a metal leash, the top half of a catch pole, a billy club, a can of Mace, and a hypodermic with acepromazine capsules in a plastic case. A .38 police special sat in a holster at the small of her back.

"Oh my God," Clare Sparrow said. She darted a nervous glance at the storeroom, which was closed.

"Let me guess," Quill said. "You have a report of a dangerous animal from a certain pointy-headed Frenchman up on the hill. Hard luck. The cat's not here, Carol Ann."

"What cat?"

"You aren't looking for a cat?"

Her candid blue eyes narrowed speculatively. "Should I be?"

"No," Quill said hastily.

"Are you talking about that big orange monster that attacked me down at your beach?"

"No," Quill said, mentally cursing her impulsive comment.

"Because I got a report. That cat's dead."

Quill glanced sideways at Clare, who smiled and gazed guilelessly back.

"Smashed flat on Route 15, is what I heard," Carol Ann said with repellant satisfaction. "That cat came to a bad end. Some responsible citizen left a message for me on the animal control hotline. And that's a good thing, because that cat was a menace, clear and simple. It was going right to the top of my ten most wanted list. It would have been number one. But," she said bitterly, "it's already dead."

"That is *so* not fair," Elizabeth Chou said mendaciously. "But I heard that, too. About the poor kitty gone to cat heaven. You've had so much on your plate this morning, Quill, that we didn't get a chance to tell you."

Nobody in the kitchen looked at the closed pantry door.

"Guess I was wrong," Quill said cheerfully. "Max isn't here, either, by the way."

Carol Ann bit her lip thoughtfully. "You mean that dog of yours?"

"That's the one. And before you ask, yes, his license is up-to-date, and no, he hasn't hit any Dumpsters lately. So don't even think about putting him on your list."

"It's only a matter of time, isn't it?" Carol Ann murmured. "Anyhow, I'm not here in any official capacity."

"Oh. Then I can't see how I can help you."

"Well, now, I'm a liar. It is official business, for sure. I mean, it is a town function, and M. LeVasque feels as I do, that the animal control officer should not be overlooked in an event as important as the Welcome Dinner."

"Oh!" Quill gave a sigh of relief. "As far as the dinner is concerned, we're drawing names out of a hat. Best of luck, Carol Ann. We'll let you know if you make it."

"Out of a hat?" Carol laughed in a sinister way. "M. LeVasque warned me that you might try to trick me out of a seat. That hat business is just a barefaced lie. I have it on the best authority that the list was made up last week, by you, Sarah McHale, and I just stopped by to make darn sure I'm on it."

"M. LeVasque is completely wrong," Quill said with unexpected firmness. "The choice is completely random and we haven't drawn the names yet."

Carol Ann's scary blue gaze swept the

143

room. "Who's in charge of it?"

Quill took one look at Dina's terrified face and couldn't do it. "I am," she said. "And as I just told you, I'll let you know as soon as the list is made up."

"When?" Carol Ann locked her eyes on Quill like a laser seeking a target.

The doorknob to the pantry door rattled. Then a furious scratching sounded at the bottom. A large orange paw hooked itself under the door and began to pull. Clare dropped the kitchen towel she'd been holding, walked casually over to the door, and rested her back against it.

"When?" Carol Ann repeated.

The scratching stopped, abruptly. A furrow appeared between Carol Ann's perfectly shaped eyebrows. "Do you hear something?"

"Bit of a mouse problem," Elizabeth said.

"Mice!" Carol Ann paled. "You do know that rodent control is not part of my job description."

"No?" Clare said. "Gosh. And we were just talking about what course of action to take before you came in. Maybe you could just take a look? There's a pretty large nest in there, and Meg's worried that they've infested the flour. I haven't," she said ruminatively, "seen mice as large as that since I lived in New York."

"Yeah, well, tough luck on you. You have a problem? I suggest you call an exterminator." She smoothed the sleeves of her T-shirt and edged toward the swinging doors. "I'll be going now. You remember what I said about the dinner."

"You bet," Quill said.

"And you can drop my ticket off at the town offices. Or my house. Whatever."

"Mm-hm."

"I'll give M. LeVasque your regards, shall I?"

"Please do."

Clare waited a few minutes after the doors to the dining room closed behind Carol Ann. Then she opened the door to the pantry to reveal Bismarck sitting in the middle of the floor. He got up and, with an offended switch of his tail, walked over to Clare, wrapped both front paws around her ankle, and bared his teeth.

"Don't even think about it."

Bismarck yawned widely, padded to the prep table, and curled himself up beneath it. Then he went to sleep. Quill wanted to curl up beside him. But the house phone rang at the little desk where Meg sat to make up the menus. Quill looked at it but didn't pick it up.

"Shall I get it?" Clare asked.

Quill's hair was starting to fall down, and it wasn't even noon. She pinned it back up in an absentminded way. "The odds are forty to one that it's some Chamber member outside in the lobby looking for one of those darn dinner tickets."

"Oh, I'll get it!" Dina snatched up the phone and said, "Kitchen. Oh, hi, Mrs. Henry. You're out front? Yes. I'll check and see if Quill's here." She put her hand over the receiver and mouthed "mayor's wife" at Quill, as if she didn't know perfectly well who Mrs. Henry was.

"Sure," Quill said, resignedly. Adela and Elmer already had dinner tickets so at least she wasn't going to be harassed about that. "Ask her to have a seat in my office. And the Chamber members are all on an e-file, aren't they? Could you print them out? We're going to have to make up this darn list and post it somewhere, or we're all going to be crazy in two seconds flat."

She went back through the dining room. At least people were coming to eat lunch. It was scarcely noon and most of the tables were full. As a matter of fact, Kathleen had put up the velvet rope at the foyer, and there were a surprising number of people waiting for tables already. Kathleen, who rarely lost her aplomb, was looking harried.

"I put in a call for more waitstaff," she said as Quill wound her way through the crowd and met her at the podium where they kept the reservation book. "There must be a couple of tour buses in town. I don't understand it. We've been busy before — but never like this."

Quill took a good look at the crowd. There were a fair number of middle-aged couples — very usual for this time of year in the Finger Lakes. But there were also a dozen or more teenagers, at least three mothers with little kids in their wake, and old Franklin Peterson, who was eighty-three and spent all of his days in the corner booth at the Croh Bar because he was scared of his wife, Arlene.

"Oh, no," Quill said. "He couldn't. He didn't." She stopped a heavyset woman in shorts, flip-flops, and a T-shirt that was having trouble covering both bosom and belly at the same time. "Ma'am? You are very welcome here at the Inn, but could I ask what brought you in today?"

"Free food," she said. "There's a sign right down to Main Street. Free three-course meal at the famous Inn at Hemlock Falls."

9

A great chef is always ready for the un-expected guest.

— From *Brilliance in the Kitchen,*

B. LeVasque

"So then what did you do?" Meg sat curled up at the end of her couch. It was after nine o'clock, and Quill hadn't been this tired in her entire life. "How many people showed up for free food again?"

"One hundred and fifty-six."

"She was absolutely brilliant," Clare said.

Meg's rooms reflected her personality in a way like nothing else could. Her sister was interested in good food, good wine, interest-ing men, and not much else. She favored jeans and baggy shirts in the winter, and shorts and baggy shirts in the summer. (She did have a wide variety of socks whose color tended to reflect her mood.) Her carpet and her furniture were beige, and almost completely covered with bright throw pillows (like the seasonings she favored in her entrees) and hundreds of cookbooks. Any space not covered by throw pillows or cookbooks had a plant on it.

Clare sat in the only comfortable chair in the room, her feet atop Julia Child's two-volume set on French cooking. Quill sat opposite her sister on the couch.

Quill looked a little blearily at them. "I locked the front door. I sent Mike down to take the sign down and then take it to the sheriff's department so Davy can have it checked for fingerprints. I walked into the dining room and told everyone that they were victims of a prank and to please bear with us while we prepared enough lunch for everyone. I called Peterson's liquor store, and Clare went and got ten cases of the cheapest wines they had and we put a bottle on every table. And then . . ." Quill swung her feet up onto the coffee table and took a healthy sip of her glass of red wine. "I called Betty Hall."

"The best short-order cook in the east," Meg said with satisfaction. "That *was* brilliant, sis."

"I asked Dina to run some vouchers off on the computer, and I gave those out to the people we had to turn away. There were a few who left without eating anything because it took so long to get rolling, but by and large, people were pretty cheerful. Especially after I got the wine and Nate brought out the beer. And Betty cooked like a maniac. I'm afraid," she added apologetically, "that we had to grind up all your tenderloin for hamburger."

"Pooh!" Meg flicked her fingers airily. She grinned at Clare. "And how did you survive all this?"

"I violated every single principle I had," Clare said. "I fried hamburgers. I fried potatoes. I grilled hot dogs and scattered potato chips like there was no tomorrow." She shuddered. "And I never want to do it again."

"I am *so* glad I missed all this," Meg said with unnecessary candor. "I would have been flattened."

"We owe Adela and Elmer your best meal, by the way. Can you believe that she came up to warn me about the sign? And you know what else? She was so mad about LeVasque's dirty trick that she threatened to cancel the Welcome Dinner."

Clare was startled. "I thought Elmer Henry was the mayor."

"In name only." Meg grinned. "Have you met the USS Adela? I'd say not. If she

150

decides to make Elmer cancel the dinner, it's as good as done."

"She marched right off to tell LeVasque off, too." Quill thought of Elmer's formidable wife with affection. "Now if we could just get Marge Schmidt after him, he'd really be toast. She could take the whole academy down with one hand tied behind her back."

"Just when you think small towns are going to drive you absolutely nuts, something like this happens," Meg said sentimentally. She set her wineglass on the table with a satisfied burp. "So now what do we do? You think it was LeVasque behind this?"

"Of course he is," Clare said. "This kind of dirty trick is right up his alley."

"And what are we going to do about it?" Meg looked brightly from one woman to the other. "If we need a good lawyer, I can recommend someone."

Quill eyed her sister. "Just what *did* you do today, Meg?"

"Oh, you know. This and that. Went to Buttermilk Falls and hiked the gorge. Justin says this is the most beautiful part of the world ever. Seeing it through his eyes, I have to agree."

"I am *so* glad you had a restful afternoon."

Meg reached over and patted her knee. "If

I'd known, I would have been there like a shot."

"You did know. I left at least six messages for you."

Meg shrugged. "I turned my cell off when I was hiking. Wasn't I here as soon as I did get the messages?"

"Yeah." Quill rubbed her eyes and yawned. "Anyhow. It's over. At least, I hope it's over."

"Which brings us back to my original question. What are we going to do about LeVasque?"

"Sue him," Clare said briefly.

"We're not very litigious," Quill said. "But I was wondering if this qualifies as some sort of harassment. He has to be breaking some kind of law. Don't you think?"

"Vandalism and malicious mischief," Meg said with that infuriating air of authority. "No question. Justin says we could have LeVasque arrested."

"Of course, there's the matter of proving it," Quill added. "I did ask Mike to take the sign over to Davy Kiddermeister in the hope that there's some sort of evidence to link him to that particular prank. But I'll bet you that last case of cheap red wine that LeVasque was careful not to leave any clue at all."

"All this must be costing you quite a bit," Clare said.

Quill made a face. "I didn't dare add it up. Just ordered food and wine with total abandon. I'm due to go over the quarter numbers with John Raintree in a few weeks, and I'll take a look at the total damages then."

"John's done our accounts for years," Meg said to Clare. "He was our business manager until he fell madly in love with my sister."

Quill took a purple throw pillow and slung it in Meg's direction. "Don't be a jerk, Meg."

"Sorry," Meg said blithely. "Anyhow, it all worked out for the best. He married a terrific woman and they have a terrific baby, and best of all, he still straightens out Quill's messes every quarter."

"You are being just a pain tonight," Quill said. "Will you cut it out?"

"It's guilt!" Meg clutched her chest. "Guilt, guilt, guilt that I'm having a fabulous time, um . . . hiking . . . while you two were forted up like those guys at the Alamo."

"Well, the Spaniards almost won this one, too," Quill said. "But not quite. And spare me any more gush about your hiking adventures, okay?"

"Myles has been away too-o-o long," Meg

said. She ducked, as Quill picked up a thick-ish volume of Jacques Pépin. "Now that would hurt. And I apologize for my inappropriate blabbing."

Clare shook her head, smiling. "I think you're in love."

"Is *that* what it is?" Quill said crossly.

"She's giddy," Clare said. "Looks like love to me."

"Well, LeVasque looks like a big, fat problem to me," Quill said, bringing matters back to the issue at hand. "And I'm ready for some suggestions on how to solve it."

"You're not interested in suing him?"

"It's tacky," Meg said.

"It's tacky and expensive, and it's cowardly," Quill said. "Plus, it takes too long."

"Hit man?" Clare suggested.

"Yeah, right," Meg said. "Next?"

"We talk to him," Quill said.

"Hm." Clare's tone was dubious. "Maybe with a two-by-four hidden behind our backs, just in case?"

"No." Quill was calm, but definite. "We'll try a reasonable, rational discussion first."

"Then the two-by-four?" Meg said hopefully.

"No hitting, no biting, no yelling. Just rational discourse."

"Okay, Kissinger. It's your funeral." Meg reached for the bottle of wine and poured herself a second glass.

Clare stood up. "Let's go, then."

"Now?" Meg set the bottle back on the coffee table.

"It's what . . . nine thirty? On Tuesday? The classes are over for the day and everyone's sitting around with their collective fingers up their collective noses listening to LeVasque rant about how they screwed up during the day."

"You have employee meetings at night?" Quill asked.

"LeVasque's a night owl."

Many chefs were, Quill knew. "Well, okay, I guess."

"He'll be as relaxed as he ever gets. And Madame will have had her ration of vodka for the day, so she'll be mellowed out some. If you're going to get anywhere with LeVasque, Quill, now's the time. His little prank's backfired on him. You do think," she added anxiously, "that Adela Henry made good on her threat to clobber him with cancelling the dinner?"

"She left word with Dina that she'd settled his hash," Quill said. "Gosh. I would have liked to have seen that."

"He may act like he's God Almighty and

doesn't give a hoot for the peasants, but you can be sure he's smart enough to know he can't get the entire village mad at him." Clare set her jaw. "I'm ready if you guys are. We'll show him he can't jerk the Quilliams around. Or the Sparrows, either."

"Okay." Quill got up, brushed off her skirt, and rewound her hair on the top of her head. "Let's roll, ladies."

"So what is it we're going to say to him?" Quill tapped the steering wheel with her fingers ten minutes later.

"Nervous?" Meg said.

"Yes. No. Sort of."

It hadn't taken any time at all to reach the academy. Quill pulled into the circular drive with the feeling that she'd been transported instantly from Meg's rooms to the big, lighted building with no time at all for reflection. Or for backing out. "What kind of mother am I, anyway?" she said aloud. "Am I a wimp? Heck no! I'm setting a good example for Jack. I'm standing up for myself. For him. And for the Inn!" She put her foot on the brake but kept the car running. "I should probably park in the lot," she said. "Not here in front. See that sign? It says: NO PARKING."

"Who cares?" Meg said. "Besides, if you

leave it here with the keys in it, we can make a quick getaway if we have to. And anyway, the guy's a bully. And you know what happens when you confront a bully."

"He gets even madder?" Quill said.

"No! He backs off and grovels. Right, Clare?"

"Right."

Meg hopped out of the car and stood on the asphalt. Quill killed the engine and got out, too. Clare led the way up the wide front steps and pushed open the big oak doors.

Inside, the place smelled of fresh paint and wood wax with a slight winey fragrance. The place was dimly illuminated, the overhead lights having been turned off for the night. The classrooms with the Viking dual-fuel ranges were directly across the lavish foyer. Meg went to the glass windows that overlooked them and peered in. "Gorgeous," she muttered between her teeth. "Damn!"

Quill peered over her shoulder. Five ranges occupied each of five workstations. Prep sinks had been built at the end of each station. Pot racks hung over each stove, filled with sauté pans and pots of various sizes.

"The knives and such are in the drawers in the middle of the workstations," Clarissa said. "You see those cameras overhead? If a student can't actually see the master chef teaching the class, it's available on camera. All a student has to do is look up."

"Words fail me," Meg said. "Where in the heck did all the money come from?"

Clare looked surprised. "You know, I'm not sure. Investors, I guess." She smiled, and Quill was struck again by how sad her face was in repose. The contrast was startling. "But if I'd paid more attention to the money end of things, I wouldn't be in the fix I'm in, would I? Anyway." She sighed. "LeVasque holds his meetings in the tasting room. It's over this way."

They followed her down the hall to another set of giant double doors. These were carved with representations of grapevines and hops.

"The man thinks awfully big, for a short guy," Meg muttered.

Clare tapped on the doors as a formality, then pressed the brass handle down and walked in.

The tasting room was as lavish as the classroom. The ceiling soared to twenty-four feet or more. The flooring was Italian marble with brass insets. Three of the four walls were covered in oak shelving specifically designed for wine. A long chest-high bar ran around the three walls of wine, with brass spigots at intervals of about ten feet.

Three long trestle tables occupied the center of the room. The academy staff sat at the middle one. Quill recognized Raleigh Brewster, Clare's henna-haired neighbor. She was a little vague on the names of the rest of the members of the academy; she knew that the older woman with a nose like a hatchet and iron gray hair folded into a tight bun was Madame LeVasque, but the employees were mere faces.

A tall, handsome man, elegantly thin, leaped to his feet as Clare came into the room. *"Cara!"*

"Hello, Pietro." Clare surveyed the table with her arms folded across her chest, her stance angry. "Where's LeVasque?"

"We thought perhaps you were he." Pietro made a face and shrugged. "He has not been seen."

"Hiding out," Clare said. "I'm not surprised. The little coward."

Quill, alarmed at the belligerent tone this meeting was already taking, cleared her throat in what she hoped was a marked manner. Clare ignored her. "You all must have heard what happened at the Inn this afternoon."

"It was a lousy trick," Raleigh muttered.

159

"And an expensive one," Clare said. "Somebody owes the Quilliams big-time for this prank."

Madame's iron gray eyebrows rose in alarm. "How expensive?" she demanded.

This was the first time Quill had ever heard Madame speak. And she wasn't French. Those flat vowels ("ha-ow expensive?") were strictly midwestern.

"You have a rough total, Quill?" Clare nudged her. "Quill?"

"Um." Quill patted her skirt pocket helplessly.

"It doesn't matter now," Clare said firmly. "What matters is that you have to do something about the Maitre, Madame."

Madame spread her hands in a gesture of grim resignation. "You know how he is."

"I know that the only person he'll listen to is you." Clare dragged a chair away from the table and swung it around, so that the back faced the group. Then she straddled the seat, sat down, and leaned her arms on the back. "This harassment of the Inn has to stop. Well?"

Madame's eyes shifted craftily. "I'm not saying he did it. And I'm not saying he didn't."

"Of course he did it. He put that sign up, he called the animal control officer, and he told those poor people at the Inn Quill had swine flu . . ."

"I overheard that," Madame admitted. "He got some bad information. I'm sorry about that."

". . . Not to mention a bunch of other crap."

Madame rubbed her hand over her considerable jaw and looked Meg and Quill over. "You two. Sit down."

Meg and Quill sat in the two chairs the farthest from Madame. Madame continued to stare at them.

"Lovely place you have here," Quill offered, as the silence stretched out.

"You're Margaret Quilliam," Madame said suddenly, ignoring Quill's attempt at social pleasantry. "Bernie thought you might come and work for us. You make a decision yet?"

Meg said, "Hah!" and folded her arms across her chest.

"Thought so." Mrs. LeVasque shrugged. "There you are, then."

Quill felt her jaw drop.

"There you are then, what?" Meg demanded. "You'll stop trying to drive us out of business if I come and cook for you?"

"Of course not. But Bernie didn't like to

be balked, and it's pretty clear you balked him."

"This is outrageous," Meg muttered between clenched teeth.

"It's an explanation," Madame said. "And once I've got an explanation, I always had ways to keep the Maitre in line."

She pronounced it "may-ter," with no attempt to soften the vowel or roll the "r." With Mrs. LeVasque, it was becoming clear that what you saw was what you got.

"Clare? I hear you're working for these two, now?" Madame jerked her thumb at Meg and Quill. "Yeah? Well, all that would do is make him madder, don't you see." This was said with an air of such kindly explanation that Quill bit her lip so she wouldn't laugh. She cleared her throat to get Madame's attention. "But neither of these things is going to happen, Mrs. LeVasque. Meg isn't ready to give up her situation at the Inn . . ."

"I'd rather be *dead*," Meg exploded. "I'd rather eat a rat!"

". . . And Clare is a wonderful addition to our staff. So we'd like to come to an understanding if we could."

Madame sighed. "I'll have to talk to him."

Quill, heartily encouraged by the burgeoning success of her negotiations, decided to press on. "Perhaps if you asked him to come and meet with us? Right now? It'd be such a relief to us all to settle this."

Madame looked around the table. "Who saw him last?"

"I thought I heard him on the phone in the office about seven," Raleigh said.

"That would have been me," Pietro said.

A man who was Chinese, compact and round-faced, raised his hand with an eager smile. He looked to be in his mid-thirties. "I'm Jim Chen, Chef Quilliam," he said. "Seafood and fish mostly. Just let me say how much I admire your way with aspic . . ."

"Which is a shot at me," snapped the aggressively drab middle-aged woman next to him. Her graying brown hair was skinned back from her forehead and pulled into a painfully tight bun. The thick lenses of her spectacles made her eyes look bulgy. "I'm Mrs. Owens. Fruits and jellies along with the fruit and veg. Not to take anything away from your aspic, Margaret, but you might think about how long you soak your gela—"

"Be quiet, Mrs. Owens," Madame said flatly. "Jim, any idea where Bernie is?"

Jim Chen shrugged.

"You have anything to add other than advice for Miss Quilliam, Mrs. Owens?"

"No, Madame." Mrs. Owens sniffed.

"Then just shut up for a while, okay? Pietro, go look in the wine cellar, will you? He's probably after another bottle of brandy."

Pietro tossed his head and said frostily, "I am not a sheep dog, Madame. If you wish to recover M. LeVasque, perhaps you would like to go yourself."

"Oh, for heaven's sake!" Raleigh shoved her chair back. "I'll go get him. The wine cellar, Madame?"

Mrs. LeVasque shrugged. "That's my best guess."

Raleigh left the room to an uneasy silence, which was not broken until they heard her scream. It was short, high, and panicked. Quill was out of her seat and rushing toward the wine cellar before she had her wits together.

LeVasque lay facedown in front of the Rieslings. A blade was buried in his neck. A piece of paper was crumpled in his left hand. And there was blood all over the beautiful stone floor.

10

~ROTI LEVASQUE~
FOR FOUR *PERSONNES*

6 pounds center-cut pork ribs
LeVasque Pork Rib Rub★
LeVasque Pork Rib Marinade★

The secret to roasting pork ribs is all in the technique, *n'est-ce pas?* It is essential to break down the tissues prior to the grilling. Rub the raw ribs with the rub. Bake in a 300-degree oven in a foil-covered pan for two hours. Brush all sides with the marinade in an attractive way. Place on a hot grill for five minutes. Turn. Grill another five minutes. Serve with panache.

★In all fine groceries and 7-Eleven stores.
— From *Brilliance in the Kitchen,*
B. LeVasque

"I keep telling you. He was already dead when I got there."

Raleigh's face was ashen, but her voice was steady. She sat in the chair she had abandoned to go search for LeVasque two hours before. Lieutenant Harker from the state trooper barracks loomed over her. He looked just like the ring-necked vultures Quill had seen on a recent National Geographic special: skinny, malevolent, and ready to feast on corpses.

Quill, Meg, and Clare were clustered at the far end of the table, with the members of the academy. Madame's face was a stone. Mrs. Owens picked nervously at her cuticles. Jim Chen and Pietro Giancava sat with their arms folded across their chests, legs extended, in attitudes of fake unconcern.

Despite herself, Quill yawned. Harker's head came up and his pale eyes found hers. Quill suppressed a shudder.

"It would have to be him," Meg muttered. They had encountered Harker before. "At least he stopped glomming on to you after he heard you married Myles."

"Hasn't made him any smarter, though." Quill rubbed her arms, although the room wasn't cold. "And if he's decided Raleigh's the murderer, nothing short of a lightning strike will change his mind. Meg, I'm so tired!"

Meg took her hand and held it. "You've had an awful day. It's been an awful night."

"Maybe I should make some coffee," Clare said. "The cops wouldn't have a problem with that, right?"

"Go and do it," Madame said flatly.

"Talk to Sheriff Kiddermeister," Quill suggested. "He's really in charge here. Harker's just trying to horn in."

"Okay." Clare got up. Davy and two of his patrolmen stood outside the open door to the wine cellar. Inside, the forensics team did their work. The body had been taken away minutes before. Quill was glad of it. She thought she could smell the metallic reek of blood among the mingled odors of wine and fresh wood.

"You okay?" Meg asked anxiously.

"I'm fine," Quill lied.

Clare stopped on her way across the polished floor and murmured in Davy's ear. He blushed bright pink and nodded. Clare touched him briefly on the arm and headed out of the room to the kitchens.

Quill sighed. She hoped Davy wasn't going to complicate things and get a crush on Clare. "But, oh, Meg, I want to go home. Did Justin say when he could get here?"

"Any minute now."

Mrs. Owens stopped picking at her cuticles. "This Justin is your lawyer friend? I hope he doesn't get us all arrested. In all those cop shows on television nothing annoys the police more than a lawyer showing up. Maybe," she said with evident satisfaction, "he'll arrest both of you and the rest of us can all go home and get some sleep."

"Shut up, Mrs. Owens," Madame said. "Why don't you think of something more productive to do?" She grinned mirthlessly. "Ask Chef Quilliam about her genius with aspics."

Mrs. Owens swelled up like a turkey cock.

"Here he is," Meg said. She waved her hand over her head. "Justin! Over here!"

"Oh my goodness." Quill sat up, her tiredness forgotten. Justin Martinez looked like Benjamin Bratt. He was tall, taller even than Myles, who was six foot two in his bare feet. His coal black hair was thick and tousled. His skin was an even, gorgeous copper. He moved like an athlete, a runner, Quill thought, since he was lean.

And he had charm or tact, or something. Harker stopped him on his way across the room with that vicious swagger that was the second worst thing about him. Or maybe the swagger was the third, Quill thought.

Coming right after his damp, lecherous hands and his conceit. The two men engaged in a lengthy conversation and, miracle of miracles, Harker nodded and let Martinez on through.

He dropped a kiss on her sister's head and extended his hand. "You're Quill."

"I'm Quill," she agreed.

"Justin Martinez." He smiled and looked at the assembled group. "And you were all present here tonight?"

"I'll introduce you." Meg stood up. Her face glowed. Quill felt very sorry for Jerry Grimsby, who was not going to like Justin Martinez one little bit.

Meg sighed happily, her hand in Justin's. "This is Madame LeVasque. The, ah . . ." She fumbled to a stop.

"Widow," Madame said bluntly. "And you don't know these people, Margaret. These are my employees now and I'll handle this. I'm Dorothy LeVasque, Mr. Martinez. My husband's the one who's headed out to the morgue in the dead wagon. The tall Italian drink of water there is Pietro Giancava. My sommelier and in charge of sauces. The inscrutable Oriental next to him is Jimmy Chen. Seafood and fish. The sourpuss glowering at Meg is Mrs. Owens. Fruits and jellies, although it's technically fruit and veg." Madame's hatchet nose twitched. "And the chief suspect seems to be Raleigh Brewster, my soup and stew expert. She's the one getting worked over by that skinny son of a bitch." Madame's nose twitched again. "Think you can do something about it? That woman's no more a murderer than I am."

Justin looked over his shoulder. "Lieutenant Harker says statistics show that the person with the body when it is discovered it usually the perpetrator."

"That's ridiculous," Quill said. "LeVasque had been dead for hours before Raleigh found him."

Justin raised an eyebrow in inquiry. "You've talked to the forensics people?"

"Harker hasn't let us move out of this corner since the police showed up," Meg said indignantly. "Not even to go to the bathroom, not until a woman patrolperson showed up, at least. So no, we haven't talked to anybody."

"Then how do you know how long LeVasque's been dead?" Justin asked. He smiled, but there was a faint furrow of worry between his dark eyes. "Private knowledge?"

Quill was already regretting her impulsive comment. "No. But he was stiff. And rigor mortis doesn't set in for eight to twelve hours after death."

She hoped Justin would leave it at that. She should have known that the snippy Mrs. Owens wouldn't.

"What do you mean, stiff?" Mrs. Owens demanded. "You're not supposed to touch the body. Everyone knows that."

"I wanted to see if he was really dead," Quill improvised. "I touched his wrist."

She'd known he was really dead. Nobody whose blood spilled out over the flagstone floor the way M. LeVasque's had been was anything but dead. But that the piece of paper he held in his hand was a clue was as clarion clear as poor Raleigh's shrieks.

She made a conscious effort to keep her hands from her skirt pocket, where the precious clue resided.

"A recipe?" Meg said. She sat at the end of Quill's bed, her knees drawn up to her chin. It was three o'clock in the morning. Meg looked like she'd just gotten up from a long, satisfying nap. The police had finally let them go just half an hour before.

"Looks like it." Quill yawned. "Aren't you exhausted?"

"Funnily enough, no."

"I'm exhausted," Quill said rather pointedly. "Aren't you tired?"

"You've had a long day," Meg agreed. She drew circles on top of the duvet with a forefinger.

"I'm exhausted and I want to go to sleep."

Meg looked up, startled. "Oh! Sure!" Then, "What did you think?"

"I think the recipe's a clue. I put it back, you understand, just before Harker showed up. But I made a copy in my sketchbook. But I also think I'm exhausted. As in it's time to put a sock in it and go to bed. I'll think about the recipe in the morning."

"Not about that. About Justin. Wasn't it terrific, the way he got us out of there?"

"It was amazing," Quill said. (Her sarcastic tone had no apparent effect on her sister.) "Except that we're going to spend tomorrow morning giving more statements to the police, which is not my favorite thing by a long shot. And — have I mentioned this before? I'm tired."

"We'd still be there if Justin hadn't talked Harker into letting us all go home."

"There wasn't a reason in the world to keep us there."

"But Justin . . ."

Quill pinched herself so she wouldn't shout. Jack was peacefully asleep in her former walk-in closet, Max at his feet. Both dog and toddler slept deeply, but she'd never get to bed if Jack woke up at this hour. "Not now, Meg. Honestly."

Meg kicked her gently.

"Okay, okay. He's gorgeous. I have to admit, before I actually saw him, that I was wondering about you deciding to . . . um . . . go hiking . . . on the first date."

"It wasn't the first date," Meg said indignantly. "I don't hike on the first date."

"I, myself," Quill said reasonably, "would not consider a client-attorney meeting at the local hoosegow a first date. But there you are. I'm funny that way." She yawned so hard she could feel her jaw crack. "Seriously, Sister. Don't you want to know him a little better before you get so . . ." She waved her hands in the air. ". . . Committed?"

"We talk about everything," Meg said, as if this were an actual response to Quill's question. "I mean, I feel as if I've known him all my life. You must have felt that way about Myles."

"I didn't even like Myles the first time I met him. Remember? That awful murder at the witch trials? He kept telling us to butt out and stop interfering with the investigation."

"But you knew, didn't you? You knew that

173

Myles was it the minute you saw him."

"If you want the absolute truth, I knew that I wanted to sleep with Myles the minute I saw him, but lust is a far different thing from love, Meggie."

Meg sighed happily and settled herself more comfortably into the duvet. "I don't know if I agree with that or not. I think that love and lust are absolutely one and the same."

"You know what? Clare's asleep on the sofa bed in your living room, right? Go wake her up and drive her crazy. Better still, tell it to Bismarck." Quill turned off her bedside light, shoved herself under the covers, and put the pillow over her head. She fell asleep to the sound of her sister flouncing out the door.

11

~Farcis a la LeVasque~
For four *Personnes*

3 tablespoons olive oil
4 small eggplants
4 green bell peppers
4 small onions
4 small zucchini
4 medium tomatoes

Peel, clean, and halve all the vegetables. Oil them lightly and set aside. Reserve the insides of the vegetables for the stuffing.

Stuffing:
Insides of those vegetables
1 finely chopped onion
2 cups ground lamb
1/2 cup chopped salt pork
2 cups cooked rice
2 garlic cloves, peeled and crushed

2 eggs, beaten
2 teaspoons thyme

Sauté all of the above for fifteen minutes in a few tablespoons olive oil. Remove from heat and mix in the egg. Stuff the shells of the vegetables with this mixture and sprinkle with Parmesan cheese. Add a handful of bread crumbs to the tomatoes and onions. Dribble olive oil over all and bake at 375 degrees for thirty minutes. This is what I call a crowd of stuffed vegetables.

— From *Brilliance in the Kitchen,*
B. LeVasque

The murder galvanized the guests at the Inn. Quill knew it would. Before she was wiser in the ways of guests, she'd worried a lot about any sort of notoriety. She wasn't worried now. It was as if the pervasiveness of up-to-the-very-second news about disasters all over the world had hardened people. In her gloomier moments (which were blessedly few, now that Jack had come into her life) Quill wondered if human beings thought life itself was a sound bite on the six o'clock news.

"And to think we had breakfast over there just yesterday," Mrs. Barbarossa marveled.

"He was walking around just as alive as the next one."

Quill didn't bother to sort this sentence out. The next one, what? "It's quite a tragedy," she said temperately. "Now, to get back to the picnic arrangements."

"Oh, whatever you think, dear. You're the experts in all matters alfresco." Mrs. Barbarossa adjusted the rhinestone brooch at her neck. She wasn't wearing the WARP T-shirt today. She was dressed in a pale pink trouser suit. Quill had caught sight of the Escada label when Mrs. Barbarossa dropped it over the back of the couch before she'd sat down in Quill's office. It clashed with the crimson peonies on the couch fabric, but then most things did.

"Of course, they're bound to suspect you," Mrs. Barbarossa said with a sapient air.

Quill looked at her, startled. "Me?"

She shook her finger playfully. "Or your sister. I heard about all those awful tricks M. LeVasque played on the Inn."

"The time of death lets us both out," Quill said pleasantly. "I was dealing with those unexpected crowds for lunch and Meg was out hiking with her lawyer."

"And that was?"

"That was what?"

"The time of death."

"Oh." Quill counted backward. Poor Raleigh had found the body at ten thirty or so. Eight hours back from that was just about two thirty. Twelve hours earlier would put the time of death at ten thirty in the morning. "It's hard to be exact about these things. But between eleven and three yesterday, I should think." Muriel Fredericks had gotten a call from LeVasque at ten thirty yesterday morning, so that she could spread the bogus news about the swine flu. So he couldn't have been dead before that. Madame herself had overheard the call.

"And you were one of the people that found him." Mrs. Barbarossa shook her head sympathetically. "It must have been awful for you."

"Yes, it was."

"In the wine cellar? I heard his body was found in the wine cellar."

"It's not a cellar, as such," Quill explained. "It's a temperature-controlled room just off the classroom kitchens. Well, you know that. You all were there yesterday morning."

"Strange," Mrs. Barbarossa mused, "that nobody found him until that evening, if, as you say, the murder occurred much earlier in the day."

"It is," Quill admitted. "As a matter of fact . . ."

"As a matter of fact?" Mrs. Barbarossa urged. Her smile was sudden and happy. "You must know that you and your sister's reputations have preceded you."

"I hope that's why you decided to stay with us," Quill said in her most gracious innkeeper manner. "My sister's talents as a chef . . ." She met Mrs. Barbarossa's hopeful blue eyes with a sudden stab of dismay. "That's not the reputation you're talking about, is it? Yes, we have had one or two unfortunate occurrences in the past. But that's where they'll remain, I'm afraid. In the past. I'm a mother now, you see. And I promised my husband I wouldn't do any more detecting. My son's only two years old, and what toddler do you know that has an amateur detective as a mother?"

"Mommy!" Jack burst into the room, his gold red curls flying. *"There is a large lion outside!"* He jumped up and down in excitement. *"You have to see!"*

"Quietly, Jack darling," Quill said. "You remember about indoor voices."

"I 'member, but I do not agree," Jack said loftily. He stood and regarded Mrs. Barbarossa with some disfavor. Ladies who looked like this pinched his cheeks. "Who is this?"

"Manners, please, Jack."

"Who is this, please?"

"I am Mrs. Barbarossa. How do you do?"

Since she showed no signs of pinching his cheeks, or any other part of his anatomy, Jack nodded agreeably. "I am Jack, and there is a lion outside."

The old lady held her hand out. "How exciting! Shall we go see it?"

"Gram says it's a very large cat. Its name is Biz and I am not to touch it." He looked doubtful. "Perhaps it is not a lion. But it's carrying p'ay, so perhaps I am right."

"Prey, indeed," Mrs. Barbarossa said with swift intelligence. "A lion is a very large cat. And of course if it is carrying prey, well, that settles it, as far as I'm concerned."

"I knew it!" Jack exulted. He slipped his hand inside hers. "So you will tell Gram she's wrong."

"If Gram is Mrs. Muxworthy, I wouldn't begin to presume."

"Don't go near the kitty without an adult," Quill warned as the two of them went out hand in hand. Then, as Clare appeared in the doorway with her food planner in hand, "Mrs. Barbarossa? Can you hang on a minute? What about the WARP picnic?"

"We're going to Taughannock Falls at noon," Mrs. Barbarossa called out. "Surprise us! Just make sure there's plenty of

180

wine." She stepped aside to let Clare into the office and the two of them disappeared around the corner.

Clare looked as tired as Quill felt. "Isn't that the guest who ordered the alfresco for six people? Should I call her back?"

"You heard her. She wants to be surprised."

"She wants a surprise, she ought to try walking into the wine cellar at Bonne Goutè," Clare muttered.

"It was awful," Quill agreed. "You know what's worse?"

Clare sank into the sofa with a sigh. "Nobody's sorry he's dead?"

"Yes. Except somebody must be sorry. Madame . . ."

"She doesn't show much, one way or the other," Clare said. "And yes, she's an in-your-face sort of person, but she's decent, at bottom. Unlike her lousy husband."

"Do you think she could have killed him?"

"Madame?" Clare straightened up. "Hm. I shouldn't think so. But you never know, do you? I mean, nobody makes you madder than a relative. And I don't care who you are, anybody can be angry enough to kill."

"I don't think that's true," Quill said.

Clare regarded her cynically. "No? Someone threatens Ja . . ."

181

Quill held her hand up. "Please don't."

"Sorry. Something like this always stirs things up."

"It sure does." Quill sat back in her chair and fiddled with the cloisonné jar that had sat there ever since she had turned this room into an office years ago. "Did you happen to notice the way she talked about LeVasque last night? I think I remember this correctly, but memory is so fallible."

Clare looked at her alertly. The change in her the past few days was noticeable. There were shadows under her eyes — none of them had gotten much sleep the last night — but the sadness in her face was gone. Clare had one of those faces that waxed and waned between conventionally pretty and complex, depending on her emotional state. The ruthless part of her art regretted the ebbing of grief in Clare's face. Quill's fingers itched for her charcoal pencil before it disappeared altogether.

Clare put her hands up to her cheeks. "Have I got flour on my face? I try to check every time I leave the kitchen, but sometimes I forget."

"Was I staring? I'm sorry. I was wondering about doing a sketch. And that's always such an intrusive thing to say to people.

Except I don't do it very often. Intrude, I mean."

"You'd want to draw me?!" Clare blushed.

"Just a thought."

Clare's blush deepened. "It wouldn't be an intrusion." She laughed self-consciously. "I'm certainly glad you intruded on Bismarck. That's a wonderful sketch of him. I'm going to get it framed. I checked you out online, you know. You don't do animals."

"Hardly ever," Quill said. "Just like the admiral in *H.M.S. Pinafore*. Art's no good unless there's tension, and most animals completely go with the flow. Even Bismarck."

An indignant meow from the foyer put the lie to this. "Jack!" Quill said and jumped to her feet. She smacked herself in the forehead. "I can't believe I let this go right by me. Some mother I am!"

She raced into the foyer, Clare at her heels. Doreen stood near the desk, her hands on Jack's shoulders. Dina peered over the desk, her eyes wide with interest. Mrs. Barbarossa stood in front of Bismarck, who crouched benignly on the beautiful Oriental rug. One of Mrs. Barbarossa's rhinestone pins lay between his paws.

Jack turned and looked at his mother with glee. "P'ay," he announced. "It is a lion, as I

183

said. Did you hear him roar?"

"I really would like that back," Mrs. Barbarossa said rather stiffly. "But every time I approach the creature, it . . . it . . . snarls at me."

"It didn't snarl," Dina said. "It meowed. There's a difference."

"Clare," Quill said firmly. "I'm sorry, but we've got to find somewhere else for Bismarck."

Bismarck turned his yellow gaze on his mistress and blinked once, slowly. Then he got to his feet, and inserted the brooch delicately between his jaws. He glanced warily around the foyer, marched over to Jack, dropped the brooch at the boy's feet and began to purr. Then he turned around and made his stately way through the dining room.

"That was so cool," Dina said reverently.

"I find nothing at all cool about that, young lady." Mrs. Barbarossa was pink with indignation. Quill didn't blame her a bit.

"P'ay!" Jack said.

He picked up the brooch and handed it to his mother who said, "Puh-ray, darling. Puh-ray."

"I'll take that, if you please." Mrs. Barbarossa plucked the brooch out of her hand.

"And I think I'll lie down a bit before the picnic."

Mrs. Barbarossa marched up the stairway. As soon as her plump figure disappeared around the turn to the second floor, Quill turned to Clare. "I'm really sorry. But I just can't risk Jack. If we could just keep him in the pantry until we figure something out . . ."

"Right." Clare walked sadly after the cat, her face averted.

"And we're off to the park, young man." Doreen hefted Jack onto her hip and went out the front door. Dina waited until everyone was clear of the foyer except Quill, then said, "You're going to force Clare to get rid of her *cat?*"

"I'm not forcing anybody to do anything."

"That cat loves Jack!" Dina said indignantly. "Have you ever actually seen that cat attack anybody?"

"No," Quill admitted. "Wait. It attacked Carol Ann Spinoza's boots."

"It's not an it, it's a he. And you've felt like attacking more than Carol Ann Spinoza's boots. You know what I think? I think that cat gets a bad rap because it's so big. It's just like Muriel Fredericks's allergies. Illusory."

"We'll find a good home for him, I'm

185

sure," Quill said feebly.

"I really, really doubt that Clare's going to give up her cat. You know who's going to find a good home? Clare, that's who. And how she's going to afford it with all those bills to pay off, I'll never know. She'll end up in a tent in Hemlock Gorge." Dina slapped her textbook closed with an air of I-am-never-speaking-to-you-again.

"Did she tell you about the debt?"

"No," Dina said in a tone just short of rude. Then, with a slightly abashed look, she said, "I was nosy. I Googled her. Once I had her real name, of course."

"But how? Oh, of course. You filed her employment contract."

"I made out her employment contract," Dina corrected her. "And boy, did she get a bad rap. That husband of hers. What a jerk! And she must have had the world's second-worst lawyer, Quill."

"Meg thinks so, too. Or rather, Justin thinks so, from what I gather."

Dina, normally incurably curious about one's love life, let this pass without a blink. "So she's gone through all that and you're going to force her out into the cold?"

"It's August."

"Even so."

Quill wanted to go upstairs and take a

186

long nap, which wouldn't do, because everybody and her brother would be knocking on her door in twenty seconds or less. That was the only real drawback to her move from the house she and Myles owned back to her rooms. The lack of priv . . . "Oh, good grief!" she said.

"What?"

"My house. Clare can move into my house."

"With Bismarck!" Dina said. "That's brilliant."

"It's empty. It's just sitting there. And why the heck didn't I think of it before?"

"Meg's been in jail," Dina said. "There's been a murder. Half the town showed up for free food yesterday. The DEC called to close the beach."

"There's that," Quill admitted. "I'll go let Clare know right now."

"Thank you for not making her get rid of her cat. And Quill?"

"What now, Dina?"

"I'm sorry I spoke rather rudely."

"Yes, well, please try not to do it in front of the guests."

She went through the dining room, followed by the curious gaze of the breakfast guests and found Clare sitting in the pantry with Bismarck. The cat was on her lap, purr-

187

ing like a berserk two-stroke engine. Her face was solemn and Quill suspected that she'd been crying. A tray of kitty litter was tucked under the shelf of Meg's preserves (Quill was fervently glad that Carol Ann Spinoza hadn't seen that). Dishes of water and kibble sat next to the fifty-pound bag of bread flour. Quill crouched down and held her hand out for the cat to sniff.

"I think it's his size," Clare said. She tickled Bismarck under the chin. "And he's a little wary of new faces. And he hates to be bullied. Like I said. He has issues." She firmed her shoulders. "I've been thinking, and of course you're right. I can't believe he'd ever harm Jack, but it's a worry to you, and we can't have that. So I've decided . . ."

Quill held her hand up. She didn't want to know whether Clare had decided to give up her job or her cat. She suspected the former. "I've got a house for you."

Clare stared at her. "A what?"

"A house. My house. I don't know why I didn't think of it before, except, there's been a lot going on. Anyhow, my husband's on assignment for several more months, and when he comes home Jack and I will move back to be with him, and then you can have my old rooms here, and I don't care if Bismarck steals the crown jewels if the queen of England is a guest as long as I don't have to worry about Jack."

"Oh my God," Clare said. "Oh, thank you. Thank you."

"It's a very pretty place," Quill said. "Although the kitchen's a disaster. We're working on it."

"I don't care if it's a tent!"

"And there's a second bedroom where you and Bismarck will be very comfortable, I think. In the meantime" — Quill got off the floor with a slight groan and glanced at her watch — "we've Davy coming to take our statements about finding M. LeVasque in the wine cellar. And then we'll take your stuff over to my place and get you settled."

The pantry door was half open, but Meg tapped on the door anyway to attract their attention. "You guys having a meeting, or what?"

"Clare's going to move into my house. So your sofa bed's up for grabs again."

Meg leaned over and scratched Bismarck under the chin. "Why didn't you think about that before?"

"Because you were in jail, we almost got arrested by the DEC, we had one hundred and twenty-six unannounced people for lunch yesterday . . ."

"And we ended up with a murder." Meg

pulled the door all the way open. "Davy's here. I told him we'd meet him in your office. I told him to walk on through. He brought a couple of his uniforms with him. They've got a search warrant, too. I expect it's for the copy of that recipe you swiped off the corpse."

"A search warrant?" Quill pulled at her hair. "What are they looking for?"

Meg shrugged. "Beats me. I told them to go ahead, but to leave everything in the kitchen exactly the way they found it, or I'd brain somebody." Then with a sublime regard for her own concerns that rivaled Jack at his best, she added, "I don't care about anything else."

"We'd better get the statements over with first. Let's go around back instead of through the dining room," Quill suggested. "In the past ten minutes, the people out there watched one cat, a weepy chef, and a policeman parade on through. Not to mention me with my hair falling over my face. It's going to put them off their Eggs Quilliam." She wound her hair up and refastened the scrunchie with a purposeful air. "We designed this place all wrong, Meggie."

Davy waited for them by her office window, with a beignet in one hand and a cup of coffee in the other. Any hope Quill had that he'd be open to nosy questions about the course of the investigations was stilled by his serious expression.

"How's the case going?" Meg asked brightly.

"This shouldn't take long," he said, rather than answering her question. "You were right, Quill. The victim had been dead long before the body was found. And the two of you" — he pointed the eraser end of his pencil at Meg and Quill — "seem to have pretty good alibis."

"*Seem* to?" Meg said, belligerently. "What? That creep Harker suspects us?"

"Harker's off on a planet of his own," Davy said dismissively.

"You've established a time of death already?" Quill asked. The Tompkins County coroner's office was fast, but it'd been less than five hours since the body had been removed from the wine cellar. And she was uneasily aware that Davy hadn't said a thing about Clare's alibi.

"The time of death's not been officially established, no. Why don't you ladies sit down?"

"Ladies," Meg muttered between her teeth. "Sure *thing*."

The three of them sat side by side on the

191

peony couch. Quill thought if they clapped their hands over their mouths in the appropriate ways, they'd look just like the See-No, Speak-No, Hear-No monkeys.

He took them over the events of the night before. They'd each made a statement separately, and Quill was a little surprised to discover that Clare hadn't seen the body.

"That's not exactly true," she amended. "I peeked over Meg's shoulder . . ."

"Which isn't too hard, given the disparity in our heights," Meg said.

". . . I saw enough." She paled a little and swallowed. "Then I went back into the tasting room and put my head between my knees."

Davy turned to a fresh page in his notebook. "That seems to cover Tuesday. Now. Just a few preliminary questions about Monday."

"Monday night," Meg said, as if she couldn't quite believe he was taking the time to go over something so inconsequential.

"That's right." Davy looked up from his notebook. Quill was suddenly reminded that he was, in fact, the sheriff, and that in the past two years he'd gotten pretty good at his job. "The three of you visited the academy that night, as well."

"Who told you that?" Meg demanded. "That old trout, I expect. Madame."

"He was there, Meg," Quill said. "Remember? You called Dina and reported a break-in."

"You never called us for a statement for that," Meg said reproachfully.

"There wasn't any crime committed," Davy said. His eyes never left Clare's face. "LeVasque was on his own property. He was within his rights to bar your door until the issue over your employment contract was settled. So I told everyone to calm down, told him not to take any of your personal property, and made an incident report. Nothing else was necessary. That's not what I'm after. I want to hear about why you went there in the first place."

Quill took a deep breath. It was all going to come out. Davy already knew Clare's married name and the series of events that drove her to sign that demented contract with LeVasque. That was clear from the intensity of his expression. If he poked around much further, he was going to come up with a motive for murder that would make Clare the prime suspect.

She only half listened to Davy's patient — but relentless — questioning. Yes, she had come to the Inn in search of her cat. No,

LeVasque hadn't beaten the cat — whoever told you that? (Quill had her money on the mean-spirited Mrs. Owens, for that.) Bismarck was perfectly fine, and while she wasn't happy about LeVasque tossing the cat out the door, she wasn't furious. And no, there wasn't really a shouting match over her employment. LeVasque was upset, but he . . .

At this point, Clare's composure failed. She put her hands over her face and didn't say anything more.

"Is there a financial penalty attached to your defaulting on your employment contract?" Davy asked.

Clare didn't answer.

"We're going to be looking into this. It's going to come out eventually. Why don't you get it off your chest now?"

Clare took her hands away from her face. "I don't have anything more to say," she said quietly.

"You're not going to help yourself by refusing to talk to me."

Clare shook her head.

Davy's voice got hard. "You're out on parole, Miss Sparrow. It's not going to take an awful lot to revoke it."

"Stop it," Quill said. "Stop this right now."

There was a perfunctory tap at the door.

It opened to reveal one of the uniformed officers in the sheriff's department. She was one of the Petersons (a founding family of Hemlock Falls, and noted primarily for the proliferation of its offspring). Quill couldn't think of her name.

"Got a match, Sheriff." She held up three butcher knives, in graduated sizes. Quill recognized them right away. Meg kept them on a magnetic strip next to the prep table.

"Those knives are from my kitchen," Meg said. She jumped off the couch and made a grab for them. "I told you to leave my stuff right where you found it, Dawn Peterson, and did you listen? Clearly not. Besides, you've only got three of the four there. Where's the other one?"

"The other one," Davy said, "was in Bernard LeVasque's back."

12

It is a thing most Frenchmen love, *un petit chat* in the kitchen. I myself cook most brilliantly to the sound of contented purrs.
— From the foreword of
Brilliance in the Kitchen:
"My Incredible Life"

Clare set Bismarck down in the middle of Quill's kitchen. The cat had a lot of confidence; Quill had to give it that. Most cats were wary of new places. She'd expected the cat to crouch and look around and then maybe run under the small oak kitchen table and peer out at his new universe for a bit. Instead, Bismarck strolled around the room with the arrogance of a sixth-grade bully in a class of kindergartners.

Quill looked at her watch. "I'm sorry we have to rush this. I want to get back for my afternoon time with Jack. And there's an emergency Chamber meeting at one, which

I'd like to avoid, but I can't since they're always held at the Inn."

Clare set the kitty litter tray, the water dish, and a bowl of food around the kitchen floor. "And you've set up a meeting with Justin Martinez . . . I appreciate this so much, Quill. Everything. Arranging for the lawyer, talking Davy out of dragging me down to the station." She looked around the kitchen. "And this, of course. I don't know why you think I deserve all this."

Quill borrowed a phrase from her sister. "Phooey." Then, to avoid more gratitude, which made her itchy, "Let me show you the bedroom."

Clare followed her up the stairs.

The house was small and old. It was constructed of cobblestone and hadn't had a lot more done to it other than a modernization effort in the sixties. The front door opened into a short hallway with a stairway to the second story on the back wall. To the left was the kitchen and dining room. To the right was the living room. The living room was Quill's favorite part of the house. The house stood on the side of a drop to a tributary of the Hemlock River and the living room windows looked out over it. Clare craned her neck as they climbed the stairs and the view from the living room disappeared.

"You can see the river from our bedroom," Quill said when she got to the tiny landing at the top. "That's right over the living room. There's a bath at the head of the stairs here." She opened the door and showed Clare a tiny tiled shower, a toilet, and a miniscule pedestal sink. "This will be yours."

"Pink!" Clare said in surprise.

"Very pink," Quill said. "Pink was the favorite color of Mellesh Peterson, or maybe it was Mrs. Mellesh Peterson. They lived here in the sixties. So all this tile is pink and your bedroom . . ." She opened the door next to the bathroom. "Is also pink. Note that sixties favorite, shag carpeting. And yes, it's black, to go with the pink walls, but that, I'm told is because Mrs. Mellesh was an Elvis fan."

"Holy crow," Clare said.

"We haven't had time to redo this room, yet."

Clare edged past her and put her suitcase down on the black shag carpeting. Then she put her hands on her hips and surveyed the garish room. "It looks like Paradise to me."

"You can see the back of the property from here." Quill went to the window. This part of the house overlooked a small lawn, kept trimmed by Mike when he could fit it into his schedule.

"All these trees," Clare murmured. "It's wonderful. The whole place is wonderful."

Quill imagined it was, compared to a prison cell.

Clare drew the shabby curtains over the view. "About Bismarck. If the worst should happen . . ."

"I'll think of something," Quill promised. "In the meantime, don't worry about it. Justin's coming in to talk to you this afternoon." She hesitated. The hordes of free-food seekers that had descended on the Inn yesterday had played merry havoc with their usual routine. Clare could have slipped out at any point in the afternoon to make the ten-minute trip to the academy and back again. "I truly don't think there's anything to worry about. Unless . . ." She made a small, meaningless gesture with both hands.

"Unless I did it?" Clare's smile was more of a rictus, but at least she made the attempt. "I didn't kill LeVasque. There's no reason why you should believe me. You don't know me all that well. And isn't there some expression about smiling villains?"

"*One can smile and smile and be a villain.* Yep. Good old Shakespeare." She searched her not-very-literary memory. *"Hamlet?"*

"Whatever. Anyhow. I'm not a villain. And I didn't kill anybody, and even though I think anyone can be driven to murder under the right circumstances, I haven't met those circumstances yet. Although God knows I've thought about it. Paul and LeVasque both."

Quill was suddenly very aware that they were alone in the house. All that stood between Clare and a bolt for freedom was Quill herself.

The door to the bedroom opened with a thud and both women jumped. Bismarck walked in. He looked around the room with approval. (Cats, Quill knew, couldn't see most colors.) He shoved his head under Quill's hand, purred loudly, then jumped on the little double bed and settled himself like the Sphinx. Clare sat down and ran her hands over his ears. "I know why Sheriff Kiddermeister didn't arrest me. It's too soon for the lab work to come back from forensics, that's why. But as soon as it does, I think I'm a goner."

Quill's breath caught in her throat. She turned the gasp into a cough.

"No, no! This isn't a belated confession! But, Quill, I used that knife yesterday to chop scallions. I'm almost sure of it. So my fingerprints are going to be all over the damn thing."

It was seeing the tears in Clare's eyes for the second time that day that got to Quill. "I've never broken a promise to Myles in my life. At least, not without a really good reason. But I can't see any other way."

"Sorry? I'm not tracking very well at the moment."

"Meg and I have got to solve this case. We've got to find out who murdered LeVasque."

"You and Meg?!" Clare burst into laughter. "Oh my goodness. I'm sorry. It's just that . . ." Clare bit her lip. "Hang on a second. Okay. I'm under control. I think. What's that line from the movie? You know, the little guy who's the accountant and the big fat guy who's the play producer? 'I'm hysterical!' "

The Producers," Quill said a little coldly.

"Oh, dear. I hope I haven't hurt your feelings. But what can you do that the police can't? I mean, they're trained investigators with equipment and labs. Not to mention they're the law and you guys aren't."

"Myles says much the same thing," Quill admitted. "And we aren't the police, of course, or even private eyes. But think about this: who knows the people and circumstances involved in this case better — the three of us? Or Davy? Or, God help us, the exceptionally horrible Harker, who's in Hemlock Falls maybe once a year? Do either of these guys have the time to find out what we can find out on our own? This isn't a drive-by shooting, or a domestic or a gang incident, or even some complicated financial riddle. This is a domestic murder and the reasons for it lie with the people we know. We've a unique perspective, and we're going to use it to find out what really happened in that wine cellar. And then we'll turn all that knowledge over to the police and let them take it from there."

"Wow," Clare said. "Good grief. Maybe you're right."

"I hope so. And I'm sorry I got nettled when you became hysterical."

"And I," Clare said generously, "am sorry I laughed." She gave Bismarck a final pat and got off the bed. "So where do we start?"

"We pool all our information, which means a meeting among the three of us."

"Okay. When?"

"I've got to make an appearance at the Chamber meeting, and Meg's in charge of lunch today while you're sitting down with Justin. My time with Jack is at four. Let's say three o'clock in Meg's room. Nobody will hassle us there."

"I can't believe you guys are riding to the rescue like this."

Quill sighed and looked at her watch. "We haven't rescued you yet. If I don't show up right at three, come down to the conference room and rescue *me*, will you? Elmer seems to have a bee in his bonnet about something." She made a face. "At least I don't have to worry about people hollering at me over seats for LeVasque's Welcome Dinner. Thank goodness that's been cancelled."

13

~BROCHETTES DE LEVASQUE~
FOR FOUR *PERSONNES*

4 beef kidneys in 2-inch cubes
1 beef heart in 2-inch cubes
1/2 cup chopped salt pork
4 very small onions, peeled
18 small Moonlight mushroom caps, cleaned and peeled
4 underripe tomatoes, cut into fourths
2 green peppers, in 2-inch cubes
2 teaspoons rosemary
2 teaspoons thyme
3 tablespoons olive oil
8 stems of rosemary

Place all ingredients in a bowl and let sit for one hour. Select four sharp skewers. String the brochettes, alternating vegetables and beef. Broil one side for five minutes and the other side for fifteen minutes.

— From *Brilliance in the Kitchen,*
B. LeVasque

She drove to the Inn in a cheerful frame of mind that lasted until she ran into Adela in the hallway that led to the conference room. "Of course we're going ahead with the Welcome Dinner," Adela Henry said majestically. "The mayor absolutely refuses to cancel."

Quill paused. She wanted to point out that the guest of honor was dead but decided against it. She was sure Adela knew that. Adela, who was nothing if not forceful, gave her a nudge between the shoulders. Quill forged ahead. They had permission to use the room from Mrs. Barbarossa, who generously agreed that since WARP was picnicking, they would have no immediate need for it.

Miriam Doncaster was already there, seated at the end of the long mahogany conference table that took up most of the space. The mayor stood in front of the whiteboard. He gave a nervous start at the sight of his wife. Since Elmer always started when he encountered Adela, Quill didn't take particular notice of this. She did take a quick moment to check out the room. She hadn't been in it for a while as the WARP members seemed to be fond of meetings. The ceilings were low, since the space had been a keeping room back in the early nineteeth century. The floor was covered in a practical gray Berber. Whiteboards lined three walls of the room. A long credenza sat at the front. Quill saw that the coffee urn was on and the cups neatly stacked.

She sat next to Miriam and greeted her with a smile. Miriam gestured toward the empty seat on her other side with a nod. Her tote bag was on it. "Howie will be here in a minute. He's sitting in on the meeting with your young suspect." The librarian admitted to her mid-fifties (Quill didn't buy that for a minute). She had large blue eyes and ash blond hair. She had a raffish sort of sexuality that had kept Howie interested for the twelve years that Quill had known them.

"She didn't do it," Quill said, flatly. Miriam had many virtues, but she was unable to pass up on a piece of gossip. And she and Howie spent a fair amount of time at the Croh Bar most afternoons. So maybe she would pass that on. "Clare's innocent."

"Howie thinks so, too," Miriam said. "Your sister, on the other hand . . ." She rolled her eyes expressively. "Really, Quill. Assault with intent to do bodily harm? My goodness."

"You know Meg."

"We all know Meg. It's a good thing she was hiking with young Martinez."

Quill refused to speculate about her sister, so she said, "I just ran into Adela."

Miriam, effectively diverted, gave Adela an appraising look. She had settled next to the hapless mayor. "Where *does* she find those outfits?" Miriam whispered.

Adela was a tall woman, and more than well-proportioned, so she was noticeable to begin with. She had a fondness for dramatic colors, big jewelry, and bouffant hairstyles. Today's outfit was a pantsuit in deep mauve with a peacock blue blouse.

"She's gone online," Quill whispered back. "And it's all your fault, you know. Your introductory computer program at the library was a big hit."

"It's time this village was dragged into the twenty-first century," Miriam said proudly. "I'm happy about the new computer service, too. You'd be amazed at who comes in to use it. And it's not just our people."

"No?"

The room was filling up. Almost everyone had come to the meeting: Harvey Bozzel (Hemlock Falls's best — and only — advertising executive) walked in with an A-frame rolled up under his arm. Mark Anthony Jefferson strolled in from the bank. Old Mrs. Nickerson from Nickerson's Hardware hobbled in on her stick. Esther West, who had closed her dress shop and reopened it as a craft store came in wearing her latest creation, a long skirt made entirely of quilting squares. Her new shop was named West's Best Kountry Krafts! Nobody was sure where the "Ks" had come from. Quill suspected they had been Harvey's idea. Most signs with an exclamation point were.

Even Nadine Peterson from the Hemlock Hall of Beauty had shown up. Marge and Harland Peterson were there, of course. Quill had never known Marge to miss a Chamber meeting, unless Harland's cows were calving. And tucked in the corner, her candid blue eyes looking for something to wreck and destroy, was Carol Ann herself. Quill counted the members up. They had more than a quorum.

Miriam's voice was low and attractive, and since it was almost lost in the rising din, Quill bent her head toward her when she thought she heard the academy mentioned.

"I'm sorry," Quill said. "Who did you say comes in to use the computers?"

"A couple of people from the culinary academy come in to use the library computer service. That crabby one, especially."

"Crabbiness seems to be a prerequisite for hiring over there," Quill said wryly. "Which crabby one in particular? Not Madame herself."

"She's got the hatchet nose, doesn't she? No, it's the other one. Jellies," Miriam added vaguely.

"Mrs. Owens."

"That's it."

Quill wrote that down in her minutes book. She knew Clare was innocent. She was just as sure that someone at the academy had killed LeVasque. She was after all the information she could get. She nudged Miriam. "How often does she come in? Mrs. Owens. To go online."

"Oh, I don't know. Quite a bit when the academy started up. Then she asked me for advice on what to buy. She comes in once in a while when she's having problems with her own PC. She's not very expert. Why do *you* care?" She caught herself. "Oh. Of course. You and Sherlock are at it again."

This was the second time today someone had slighted her detective abilities, and Quill bridled a little. "I wouldn't call it 'at it again,' as such."

"I thought you promised Myles you'd butt out of this stuff."

"I agreed to temper my activities."

"Temper, huh."

"And besides. Meg's Watson."

"What?"

"I said, Meg's Watson. I'm Sherlock."

Quill looked up to see the Chamber members staring at her. Marge Schmidt winked, very deliberately.

Elmer scowled and brought the gavel down on the mahogany tabletop. Esther moved the gavel rest under his hand and went "tsk!"

Things were off to a familiar start.

"I call this emergency meeting of the Hemlock Falls Chamber of Commerce to order." Elmer whacked the gavel again, for emphasis. "Can we have a reading of the minutes?"

Quill flipped to the page labeled *July Mtg Mins.* Her chief flaw as secretary was forgetting what her contractions meant. She was relieved to see that the heading at least, was clear. The rest of it was problematic. "Hm!" Quill said, as if she were deciding where to start first.

Miriam rolled her eyes and raised her hand. "I move that we forgo the reading of the minutes."

"Seconded!" Marge boomed.

Elmer got to whack the gavel again. "So

moved. We have old business now, Quill, so we'll get right on to that."

"Those parking meters in front of my restaurants," Marge said. "That's the old business we have to talk about. I move we rip 'em up and send 'em to the dump."

Elmer's lower lip jutted out. "Now, look here, Marge."

Harland jerked awake (Marge had jabbed him in the ribs). "I second the motion," he said.

"All in favor?" Marge said.

All who had a business on Main Street raised their hands. Quill counted them off. Nadine, of course, and the Nickersons. Esther West had her hand raised, too. "This is an illegal motion!" Elmer said. He began to whack the gavel with monotonous regularity; Esther moved the rest every time he banged it down. It looked like a particularly manic version of Whac-A-Mole. Tickled, Quill began to sketch it.

"You gonna count these votes, or what?!" Marge shouted. She leaped to her feet, her right arm straight up in the air. "I'm counting, so shut up, you all." She stopped, momentarily, to whisper under her breath.

Then she sat down again.

"I guess that means the motion's defeated," Elmer said with ill-concealed satisfaction.

"We'll see about that."

Quill sketched a pissed-off Marge, out for revenge on a hapless Elmer.

"Now, if we can just get to the real old business. About this Welcome Dinner."

Carol Ann Spinoza raised her hand. "There's some old, old business before this Welcome Dinner," she said in her icky little voice. "And if we had a secretary who took the right kind of minutes, we would know that we have to take the old business in the proper order."

"That's all you wanted to say?" Elmer asked. Even though Carol Ann was no longer tax assessor, everybody Quill knew was still afraid of her. The woman had some evil power that no one could quite put a finger on.

"Of course that's not all I wanted to say. We have to vote on the most-wanted list for the post office."

Elmer looked confused, then extremely anxious. "You're with the FBI, now?"

A ripple of unease went through the room.

"The animal offenders list, Carol Ann means," Adela said with a tight smile. "Isn't that right?"

"That is exactly right. We agreed that the

most dangerous animals should be posted so that the citizens of our village could be made aware at all times of the dangers." She paused, as if to reconsider the number of times the relevant word had appeared in her sentence. "Danger," she said precisely. "That is the term."

Elmer shrugged. "Okay, I guess. You want a vote on whether or not to put this list up?"

Carol Ann's eye turned a very dangerous shade of blue. "We voted in a special ordinance two and a half months ago. I would think that the post of mayor in a town like ours would have some sort of intelligence testing before a person was allowed to run for office. Hm!" Carol Ann stopped herself in mid-stride. Her eyes brightened. She unclipped the notepad from her weapons belt and made a note. "That is a very good idea. An IQ test." Then she swept on. "The post office is part of the federal government and you can't just post anything there. So it was voted in. I made the sign." She smiled a blindingly white beauty-queen smile at Harvey, who winced. "With some help. Harvey?"

Harvey smoothed his gelled hair back with both hands and stood up. Harvey was tall, willowy, and favored pastel-colored shirts. His advertising agency was mainly concerned with the layout and distribution of the local PennySaver, but anytime anyone had any product to promote, Harvey was the go-to guy. Quill let him handle the advertising for the Inn (although she did the layouts herself).

He set the A-frame he'd carried into the meeting onto the table and unrolled it. The sign was in black, white, and red and the biggest word was DANGER, which was in red. Under that, in black type was MOST WANTED (BROUGHT TO YOU BY THE HEM-LOCK FALLS DEPARTMENT OF ANIMAL CONTROL). Underneath was a series of blurry pictures. The first one said, RABID FOX, the second RABID RACCOON. Quill fol-lowed the rest of the titles until the second to the last one, which was Max (GARBAGE RUMMAGER), and the very last one, which was Esther West's little poodle (ANKLE BITER). The final sentence was: IF YOU SEE ANY OF THESE ANIMALS THAT ARE MOST WANTED, CALL 1-800-DAN-GERS.

Esther West smoothed her spit curls and said meekly, "I'd like to register a protest."

"Me, too," Quill said. "Esther's poodle is not an ankle biter. And Max hasn't rum-maged in a Dumpster for years." (This wasn't true.) "Anyway, doesn't an animal have to be convicted, or something, before it goes onto that list?"

Esther nodded vigorous agreement. "You can't just smack any poor pet you want to onto that poster, Carol Ann. They have to be convicted."

Miriam raised her hand. "I move we table the discussion of this poster until we determine the legality of the listings."

Quill raised her hand. "I second that."

The motion was passed, although nobody's hand was raised very high and Carol Ann sat down with a poisonous grin.

Elmer sighed, as though the weight of the world was on his shoulders. Carol Ann had a long, long memory and a taste for revenge. "Can we get to this dinner, now?"

Miriam raised her hand.

"The chair recognizes Miriam Doncaster. What about it, Miriam?"

"I move we cancel the Welcome Dinner."

"I second," Marge shouted.

Elmer ran a finger around his shirt collar and coughed nervously. "Now, Margie, Miriam, that would be an idea, for sure, but I think we should have a good, old-fashioned discussion about this. That's what these meetings are all about, anyways."

A discussion, of sorts, took place. Marge shouted. Miriam protested in a ladylike way, and Harland kept asking why they wanted to welcome a fellow who was dead, which was Quill's own take on the matter.

She flipped to a fresh page in her notebook and drew a battlefield with land mines in it. Then she sketched Marge's face on one mine, Miriam's on another, and Adela's on a third. Then she put in a little Elmer tiptoeing through the field.

". . . Because I already paid him, that's why!" Elmer said. "And I tried to get the money back from the widow herself, and she said a contract's a contract."

There was a shocked silence. (Which had to be a first for a Chamber meeting.)

"Her husband was killed yesterday and she wants to go ahead with this thing on Friday?" Mark Anthony Jefferson looked as if he might be reconsidering the Bonne Goutè mortgage.

"That widow is *not* behaving in what I would call a respectful way," Nadine said, finally.

"That's right," Elmer said.

"We could turn it into a memorial," Harvey suggested.

"You mean all that money's lost, that's what you mean," Marge said. "Just to be clear about this. That woman took the check and whether or not we have the dinner, she's going to keep it?"

"That's right."

A look of admiration passed over Marge's face and was gone. "Then Harvey's right. We have to have the damn dinner. So we'll make it a memorial. With lots of dancing."

"I could do a banner," Harvey said. "Very tasteful. *Rest In Peace, Bernard LeVasque,* with maybe the most famous of his dishes drawn in the borders."

"That'd be some kind of turkey recipe, then," Marge said. "Well, this is just peachy. What the heck, the food'll be good."

"They don't have a head chef," Miriam pointed out. "And their pastry chef is working somewhere else." She glanced sideways at Quill. "What they have left is vegetables, fruits, seafood, and jellies. Not what I'd call a well-balanced menu."

"They're all cooks. Let 'em cook," Elmer said.

"At a hundred dollars a plate?" Miriam shook her head. "I'm not happy with that. Not at all. If we're paying a hundred dollars a plate, we ought to get the best chef in the northeastern United States."

Everybody looked at Quill.

Quill tucked her charcoal pencil away. "Okay. I'll ask her."

Miriam leaned over and hissed in her ear, "Go get 'em, Sherlock."

14

~CHEVON A LA LEVASQUE~
FOR SIX TO EIGHT *PERSONNES*

4 pounds goat shoulder and leg in 2-inch
cubes
1 teaspoon rosemary
1 teaspoon thyme
2 teaspoons kosher salt
3 cups lima beans
2 tablespoons olive oil
1/2 cup salt pork, chopped
2 medium onions, sliced
2 medium carrots, sliced
3 rutabagas, chopped into 1-inch cubes
2 medium tomatoes chopped into small bits
3 celery stalks with leaves, chopped
2 Turkish bay leaves
2 cups white wine
Mint for garnish

Rub the salt and herbs over the goat
meat. Sauté the goat with the salt pork

and the olive oil. Put all ingredients together and simmer for one hour in a covered pot. Garnish with mint.

— From *Brilliance in the Kitchen,*
B. LeVasque

"They want me to take charge of the kitchen?" Meg ran both hands through her short dark hair, so that it stood up in spikes.

"It was Miriam's doing. She approves of our investigation. Which means Howie's worried, I think, that maybe Davy's going to come to the wrong conclusion." Quill squared up her minutes pad onto the tabletop. They were squeezed around Meg's miniscule table. One of the first things the sisters had designed when they remodeled the old inn was their own quarters. Quill made her own rooms into a refuge; Meg made hers into a retreat. Meg's didn't have a kitchen. And since she didn't have a kitchen, she didn't need a table except to heap cookbooks on. Quill had stacked them all on the floor.

"Miriam," Meg said. "Well, well."

"Who's that?" Clare asked.

"Howie Murchison's girlfriend," Meg said.

"The town librarian," Quill said at the same time.

"Howie is the senior partner in Justin's law firm. He has a girlfriend?" Clare looked a little disappointed, which would please Howie enormously.

Quill smiled. "I see you're on first-name terms already." Howie hadn't turned up at the Chamber meeting after all. Quill guessed that he'd sat in on Clare's interview with Justin for the whole time.

"He's a nice guy." Clare shifted uncomfortably in the chair. "Very reassuring kind of guy."

This was true. Even if he hadn't been a very good lawyer, which he was, Howie looked the part. He was of middle height, with a noticeable bald spot and a small belly. Quill knew for a fact he'd worn the same pair of expensive loafers for ten years, before Miriam threw them out in exasperation.

"Did he give you any opinions?"

Clare bit her lip, but she said steadily, "He thinks I might be arrested. Certainly taken in for questioning. He told me up front that he was the judge for this county, and that he'd have to recuse himself if there was any possibility of a trial. I said, okay."

"But you were here helping me all afternoon the day LeVasque was murdered!" Quill said. "You have an alibi."

"They've come closer to the actual time of death. LeVasque was killed between one and two o'clock."

Quill sat back and said, "Damn."

"Right. I volunteered to go down to Peterson's liquor and pick up those cases of cheap wine."

"You weren't gone more than half an hour," Quill said. "And you came back with six cases of red and six of white. I can swear to that."

Clare looked away. "Can you really? You were all over the place. Kitchen, restaurant, your office . . . Howie said a decent prosecutor could make mincemeat of your testimony."

"Harry Peterson can say that you came right in, picked up the order, and came right out!"

"And where was I before I got to the store? Where did I go right afterward?" Clare took a deep breath. "There's worse to come."

Neither Meg nor Quill said anything.

"I did go up to the academy. Just for a minute. I was so furious at that little sh . . . that jackass, for pulling that dirty trick that I did want to kill him. I wasn't really going to kill him, of course. I just wanted to give him what for."

"And somebody saw you?"

"Somebody did. Mrs. Owens."

Quill digested this very bad news for a moment. Then she said irritably, "Doesn't she have a first name?"

"If she does, no one's heard it before. I suppose it's on a birth certificate somewhere." Clare attempted a smile. It didn't work.

Quill wrote *Mrs. Owens???* in big caps on her pad. "What did you do exactly? When you got there?"

"I walked in the front door. Somebody's usually on reception, but there wasn't anyone there. I walked up to the tasting room doors. They were closed. That means a tour group. I walked back to the reception desk. Mrs. Owens came down the hall . . ."

"From where, exactly?" Quill was drawing a map of the first-floor layout.

"Right there." Clare put her finger on the east side of the building. "The washrooms."

"Then what?"

"I asked her where LeVasque was. Actually, what I said was, 'Where is that little shit?' "

"And what did she do?"

"She said she hadn't seen him. I looked at the clock over the desk, realized I had to get back here and I left. And no, I don't think anyone else saw me. Just Mrs. Owens." A tear trickled down her cheek. "I was just so *mad.*"

Quill doodled for a minute. Then she flipped to the last page in her sketch pad. "Do either of you recognize this recipe?" She laid it on the table.

"Six eggs," Meg read aloud. "Two and two-thirds cup canned coconut. Three cups puffed rice cereal. One package mars . . ." She sat back. "Mars? Mascarpone? What?"

"I don't know. This was on a scrap of paper in LeVasque's hand."

"You pried his cold dead fingers open and got it out?" Meg grinned. "That's my sister."

"That's not a recipe," Clare said.

Quill raised her eyebrows. "It looks like a recipe."

Meg rolled her eyes. "What she means is it isn't food."

Quill looked at the recipe again. "Eggs are food, cereal's food . . ." The penny dropped. "Oh. You mean it's not gourmet food."

"Have I ever told you how much I hate the word 'gourmet'?" Meg demanded passionately.

"Not that I recall," Quill said.

"There's *food,* that is, delicious, nutritious, wonderful *food,* and then there's stuff like this." She flicked the paper with a

223

contemptuous finger. "I wouldn't serve a farm animal stuff like this, much less a human being."

"You are so right," Clare agreed. "What's worse, I'll bet you fifty cents that 'mar' means marshmallow. One ten-and-a-half-ounce package of marshmallows."

"Oh my God," Meg said. "I'll bet you it is. Gaah!"

Quill, who was fond of marshmallows and even fonder of puffed cereal with a little cream and lots of raw sugar, dragged matters back to the point. "So what was this doing in LeVasque's hand?"

"Beats me," Clare said.

"Maybe it's part of a poison pen letter," Meg said. "You know: dear Chef LeVasque, cook this, you bozo! Sort of like giving him the finger. Did the scrap of paper look like stationery?"

"It was from a yellow pad. The ones with lines. There are probably five million lined yellow pads in the northeastern United States alone."

"So what do we do now?" Clare asked anxiously.

"We go undercover at Bonne Goutè. Or rather, you two do. I can handle things on my own here for the rest of the week. The party's Friday, right?" She frowned. "That doesn't give you two a whole bunch of time."

"The menu was posted Sunday night," Clare said. "So the fresh stuff's been ordered. I imagine everyone's been working on their part of the meal. I was supposed to do tarte pêche, for example. And of course, I haven't done a thing about it."

"I've got a copy of the menu somewhere around here." Meg got up and began to rummage in the pile of papers stacked on her coffee table. "I'll make a list of the ingredients and see what we can come up with. It's too late to order anything in quantity, so I'll just have to cope. I remember thinking there was a real challenge in there."

"I don't suppose you'd just want to follow his original menu?" Quill said tentatively. "It'd leave you more time to investigate."

Meg didn't bother to dignify this with an answer. She dug into an accordion file and emerged with the invitation to the Welcome Dinner. "Here it is! Yep. I was right. Goat. Goat and quail."

"Goat?" Quill said, who hadn't paid attention to the menu at all. "I don't think the Chamber members know about the goat."

"It's a locavore menu," Meg said. "Only

225

local foods. It's called chevon, of course, to sneak it past the people who're put off by the idea, but it's actually very delicious. And really good for you. Chevon roti. Hmm. He meant to roast it. Idiot. It's much better braised."

"Come to think of it, neither Miriam nor Howie was hounding me for tickets," Quill said. "So at least a few of the Chamber members know about the goat." She shook herself. "Anyway. Here's what we need to do. I thought we'd take a logical approach here, and divide our investigation into three categories: means, motive, and opportunity."

"Sounds good," Clare said nervously, "except that the person with the means, motive, and opportunity is me."

"Yes, well. We'll exclude you, of course. Let's begin with opportunity. Who was at the academy between the hours of one and two that day?"

Clare made a face. "About a hundred day-trippers in the tasting room, for starters."

Quill beamed at them. "And who among them had a chance to snatch the weapon from our kitchen?"

Clare smiled. "They all came in from Buffalo on a tour bus that morning. But there was a class earlier in the morn—"

Quill, eager to make her point, interrupted

her. "So we can rule out the day-trippers."

"But what about the breakfast class?" Clare insisted. "Your WARP people or the urps or whatever they're named. They came in for Basic Brunch Techniques."

Quill rubbed her forehead. "Hm. But they hadn't met LeVasque before, had they?"

"Probably not."

"Still . . ." Quill thought a minute. "Meg, you missed the butcher knife when?"

"Monday night. Around eight thirty."

"And you, Clare, when did you last use the knife?"

"Monday night, around eight o'clock."

"And who, other than the three of us was in the kitchen?"

Meg ticked the names off on her fingers. "Mike, Carol Ann, Devon, Mallory . . . and the miserable son of a gun himself."

"LeVasque. Right. So what are the odds that LeVasque himself took the knife?"

"But, why?" Clare asked.

Quill shook her head. "We don't know that, do we? But I can think of a couple of reasons right off the bat."

"You're bluffing," Meg scoffed. "Why would he steal a knife from my kitchen?"

"He was in the middle of a dirty tricks campaign, wasn't he? My first thought is he wanted the knife to set you up for something awful. His fingerprints weren't on it, were they?"

Clare shook her head. "Not as far as I know."

"We should make a note of that, just in case." Quill wrote *knife fgprints DK????* on her notepad.

"That little bastard," Meg marveled.

"Now, now." Quill looked at the growing list in satisfaction. "Okay. Now, when you guys go undercover at the academy . . ."

"Should I dye my hair?" Meg asked sarcastically.

"Shut up. You need to find out where these staff members were."

"Which staff members?" Clare asked.

"The ones who hated his guts," Meg said.

"Everybody hated his guts."

"We'll start with the most obvious motives," Quill said. "If we have to move on down to the guy who mows the lawn or the people from WARP, we will. And you can help us here, Clare. Who hated him the most?"

"Me," Clare said promptly. "He was blackmailing me, or as good as. But after me? Madame, I suppose."

"Why would she wait to kill him after all these years of marriage?" Meg asked. "Why not, like, right after the honeymoon?"

"They had a huge fight over money Sunday afternoon. He spent a lot. He drew a whole slug of cash out to buy that Mercedes a couple of months ago and he'd drawn a whole bunch more out earlier in the week. Madame was livid. Told him if he took any more she was going to divorce him."

"Good," Quill said. "I'm putting a star after her name." She put down her pencil and looked at them. "Which brings me to something important. Did any of you notice how she talked about him last night?"

"Coldly," Clare said.

"With indifference," Meg said.

"In the past tense," Quill said. "Didn't she? Didn't she say 'I had' and 'he was.' *How did she know he was dead?"*

"Wow." Clare blinked at Quill. "You're really good at this."

"Not at all," Quill said modestly. "Okay. Who else have we got for suspects?"

"Pietro Giancava, the sommelier. He does cheeses, too. He had a green card. I know for a fact that LeVasque threatened to send him back to Italy if he complained about his salary one more time. And his green card is due to expire at the end of the month. Madame wanted to keep Pietro on. He's a wizard at picking good reds. And he's got a great palate for cheese."

229

"Raleigh Brewster?"

"Raleigh's a friend of mine," Clare said, her color rising. "She could no more stick a knife in somebody's back than . . . I don't know what. Anyhow, she didn't kill him."

"We need to rule her out, at least," Quill said gently. "You never know where these things are going to go. What if the police discover she had a motive? We can't just exempt her because of a feeling."

"You're exempting me because of a feeling." Clare looked from Meg to Quill and back again. "By God, you aren't, are you? I can see it in your faces."

Meg covered Clare's hand with her own. "There was one incident here at the Inn, years ago. Quill and I made a very good friend." She paused. "Anyhow, it turned out badly."

Clare set her jaw. "I suppose you turned this person in?"

"We'll tell you the story sometime," Quill said. "And no, we didn't. We didn't have to."

Clare sighed. "Right. So I turn rat fink on my good friend Raleigh. You haven't met her yet, but Raleigh has a daughter. She's off for orientation at Ithaca College this week. She's cute. Really cute. She hit eighteen in July, and LeVasque hit on her."

"Hit on her?" Meg said. "Like, how do you mean?"

"From what I can gather, it was just a grope and a lewd suggestion. But Divia's back for Labor Day weekend, and then she'll be back during school vacations, and Raleigh was worried sick."

"The man was disgusting," Meg snorted.

Quill looked at the names on her list. "Jim Chen?"

Clare shook her head. "Can't think of a thing, there. Jim and Mrs. Owens don't get along, but she really asks for it. Jim himself gets along with everybody. LeVasque called him names, and Madame herself never heard the term politically correct, but then, the two of them treated all of us that way. And it isn't as if Jim can't find another job. He gets better offers all the time. But his family's here in Ithaca, and he loves the area."

"Put two stars next to Chen's name," Meg said to Quill.

"On the theory that the least likely person did it? If the least likely person turns out to have done it, we've really messed up this investigation. Nope. We get results by proceeding in a methodical way, and that's what we're doing. We'll move Jim to the bottom of the list."

"Motherhood has made a *huge* difference in this woman," Meg said to Clare. "Huge."

"Mrs. Owens," Clare said. "She's my favorite pick."

Quill poised her pencil over her list. "Motive?"

"I wish I could come up with something. Anything. But if you want the truth, I think she had something on him, and not the other way round. She's lousy at her job. The very idea of that woman giving *you* advice on condiments is laughable, Meg. And she's lazy. Not to mention mean. I have no idea why LeVasque kept her on. She had every reason to keep him alive, well, and signing her paychecks. She couldn't get a job at a truck stop."

Quill, who had eaten at one or two very good truck stops in her time, made a note: no obvious motive. "Okay. We're ready. When do you two want to start?"

Clare got up and began to collect her things. "I think I'll get over there right now, if there's nothing you need me for tonight, Meg."

"Nope. I'll get Bjarne and Elizabeth set to cover me for the next three nights, and then I'll come by and join you. We'll need a meeting of the staff tonight anyhow, so I can reset this menu."

"Has anyone talked to Madame?" Clare asked. "She doesn't mix much in the kitchen affairs, but she is head of the academy now."

"Elmer and Adela went to negotiate with her. I'm pretty sure she'll . . ." Quill broke off at the sound of a knock at Meg's door. "I'll bet that's Doreen and Jack."

It wasn't. It was Dina, and she didn't look as if she brought good news.

"Sorry, guys. But Davy's downstairs with that horrible Lieutenant Harker." She bit at her lower lip and then took a deep breath. "I'm afraid they're asking for you, Clare."

15

A great chef prepares a meal as a play-wright prepares to entertain. Act 1 is the hors d'oeuvres. Act 2, the entree. Act 3, the dessert. I, myself, as Shakespeare only occasionally does — prepare my menus in five acts. Hors d'oeuvres, the soup, the fish, the meat, and as an entr'acte, the salad. The final act is the dessert.

> — From the foreword of
> *Brilliance in the Kitchen:*
> "My Incredible Life"

"We're keeping well out of the way of the police investigation, Myles." Quill adjusted the pillows behind her back and cupped the cell phone closer to her ear. Outside her bedroom window, the early sun flooded the vegetable garden with pale gold. "But I did want you to know what's going on." The reception was so clear that she could hear the concern in his voice. Concern, tinged with slight exasperation.

"I'll put a word in about Harker," Myles said. He didn't say to whom. He never did.

"Now you're sounding grim. Whatever word you put in last time I had to deal with him seems to have had a lasting effect. I'm fine. I mean, he's still the creepiest guy in Tompkins County, but he isn't hassling me. And I'll tell you something really good. Davy's growing into the job. I know you said he would, eventually, but I hadn't really noticed until now. He's going to be a good sheriff, Myles."

"I miss you," he said suddenly.

Quill felt her throat tighten. "I'm getting sentimental after three years of marriage," she said lightly. "If you say anything else, I'm going to weep."

"Yes, well." He cleared his throat. "It shouldn't be too much longer before I can get back."

"Don't give me a date," Quill said. "I'll just obsess over it. Are you ready to talk to Jack? You've had a chance to look at the pictures I e-mailed last night? Well, it's this morning, for you, isn't it?" He didn't answer that, either.

"I liked the pictures a lot," Myles said simply. "But the one with Jack asleep . . .

that's a beauty. But where the devil did that cat come from?"

Quill looked at Bismarck, who was peacefully curled up at the foot of the bed. "That's Clare's cat. Meg brought him back here last night, to keep in her room while Clare's lawyers get this jail thing sorted out. When I checked on Jack last night, the cat was curled up with him, purring like anything. I think we might have made a mistake using door levers instead of knobs. He just stuck his paw up, pulled the door levers down, and walked right in. Bismarck, I mean. Not Jack. Anyhow — Doreen doesn't lock up until I get in, and Meg never locks up at all, so I guess he took advantage."

Jack appeared at the bedroom door, his bronze red hair floating around his head like a halo. Bismarck yawned and sat up. "Lion!" he shouted, gleefully. He marched toward Quill's bed like a tiny, determined missile. Quill waved the cell phone in the air. "It's Daddy, Jack."

"Daddy!" Jack leaped on Quill, pulled the indifferent Bismarck's tail in greeting, and grabbed the phone. He held it in front of him like a microphone and shouted, *"Daddy?* We have a lion and it's here to stay!"

Quill reached over, pressed the conference

call button, and Myles's voice flooded the room.

"You been crying?" Doreen demanded twenty minutes later. Her old friend looked at her with concern. Then she stooped and took Bismarck's toy mouse out of Jack's mouth. She set it down in front of the cat, who looked at it with disdain, as if to say, "Kid slobber is not my thing."

Quill drew her knuckles under her eyes. She was mostly dressed, except for her shoes. She pulled a pair of sandals out of the cabinet under the microwave and slipped them on. "Yes," she said. "I miss Myles. I miss not having the family complete."

"You're going to miss those urp people if you don't get downstairs," Doreen said in a pragmatic way. "They're all checking out."

"They can't do that!" Quill bundled her hair on top of her head and looked around for a scrunchie. "They were supposed to stay until . . ." She thought about it. "They were scheduled to leave today, weren't they? They were here for a week, and they checked in last Thursday and this is Thursday. Well, they can't leave, that's all."

Doreen took a scrunchie out of her apron pocket and handed it over. "I don't see why not. It's a free country."

"But they might be suspects!"

"You mean one of them might have skewered the Frenchman?" Doreen's lower lip stuck out, a sign of disapproval. "I thought you told Myles you were through with that kind of goings-on."

"Myles knows all about it." Quill patted her skirt pockets, found them empty, and hastily distributed her sketch pad, her keys, sunscreen, and her charcoal pencil between them. "It's a remote possibility, I'll admit. They don't even know the guy. But don't you think their leaving now is suspicious?"

"Not if they booked the Inn for a week and the week is up. Of course the police might want to keep them here, too." She darted a look at Jack. "Because of the second M-U-R-D-E-R. Last night."

Quill stared at her. "Because of the what?!"

"The second M-U-R . . ."

"Stop that," Quill said crossly. "I heard you the first time. Do you mean there's been another death?"

"I was waiting for the chance to tell you," Doreen said with a long-suffering air. "But you were on the phone with Myles, and then you were in the shower, and then you were flying around here like you usually do."

Quill crouched down and addressed her son. "Jack. I want you to go into your room and play with your toys for just a second, okay? Mommy needs to talk to Doreen."

"No," Jack said with a huge smile. "I think not. No, no."

"Okay," Quill said. "I don't want you to go near your room today, okay? Don't go in it at all. Stay out, out, out."

"Okay," Jack said cheerfully. "I'm going to my room, now. Come on, Biz."

"Jack," Quill began. She looked at the cat. The cat looked at her. ("And I swear," she said to Myles later, when the whole case was over, "that cat winked at me.") "Fine," she said. "Don't play with your toys, now. Especially the Ding Dong School Alphabet Game."

"Ohh-*kay!*" Jack said. He trotted into her bedroom. Bismarck yawned widely and waddled after him.

"That worked a treat," Doreen said admiringly. "I'll have to remember that."

"What I want you to remember is why you didn't tell me about this right away," Quill said with a certain sternness. "Has there been another murder?"

"That Mrs. Owens. Last night. Somebody coshed her on the head and stabbed her to death to boot."

Quill put her hand to her lips. "Oh, no. Oh my gosh. This is just terrible."

"It sure is," Doreen agreed.

"Where did it happen?"

"Peterson Park," Doreen said. "By that big ugly statue of General Hemlock. They figure she was there to meet somebody. They figure . . ."

Quill was already out the door. She hurried down the two flights of stairs to the foyer and stopped at the bottom tier. Her first thought was, *There are too many people in the entryway.* Her second thought was, *My gosh, they're arresting Big Buck Vanderhausen.*

The lobby was small, and it wasn't designed to accommodate the five members of WARP, three policemen, Dina, Meg, Mike, and a few people with napkins clutched in their hands who had wandered in from the dining room. Patrolwoman Peterson had her hand on Buck Vanderhausen's shoulder. Vanderhausen's hands were cuffed behind his back. He looked really, really angry. Davy Kiddermeister had his head down as Mrs. Barbarossa whispered urgently in his ear.

There was also a lot of luggage.

Quill reached the bottom of the steps and

tried for a stern, authoritative voice. "What in the name of goodness is going on here?" The only person who paid any attention to her was Meg, who had her tote bag over her arm and her case of knives at her feet.

"About time you came down," she said. "I sent Doreen up to tell you what happened hours ago."

"It's barely seven thirty," Quill said. "And Doreen comes at seven. Besides . . ." She shut herself up. "What happened?"

"I was on my way over to Bonne Goutè when Davy showed up. Asked if we had an Arnold Henry Vanderhausen registered. Dina's been so spooked by putting me in jail for a couple of hours that she wouldn't tell him a thing. And she didn't want to trouble you, because it's Thursday morning and Myles always calls on Thursday. Anyhow." Meg paused and took a deep breath. "So she came and got me, and I got Vanderhausen, and everyone seems to think he killed Mrs. Owens. Vanderhausen," she added in case Quill hadn't gotten the point.

"Why do they think that?"

"He has this whacking big bowie knife, right? Well, it was found in Mrs. Owens's chest."

"So he didn't do it."

"Probably not. Not even a Texan would

241

be that dumb."

"Why are you casting aspersions on Texans?"

"Because I'm scared and pissed off and I have to pick on somebody." Meg shifted her tote from one shoulder to the other. "He's got a record, by the way. According to Dina, who had it from Davy, he served time for armed robbery. A gas station, I think." Meg sighed heavily and shifted her tote back to her other shoulder. "What a mess. Do you suppose he killed LeVasque, too?"

"Why?"

"Money, I suppose. It's the usual motive in stuff like this."

"But LeVasque wasn't robbed of anything."

"Do we know that for sure?"

Davy raised his voice. "All right, everybody. Show's over. If you would all go back to what you were doing, I'd appreciate it."

Quill stepped forward. "Davy, I mean Sheriff Kiddermeister . . ."

"Not now, Quill, okay? You have any questions, I'll get around to you later." He nodded to Officer Peterson, who put one hand on Vanderhausen's head and guided him out the door. Mrs. Barbarossa, her face pale under the dabs of blusher on her cheeks, gestured feebly to Quill. She stood at the center of the remaining members of her group. William Knight Collier looked as if he'd just received notice of an audit by the SEC. The Frederickses looked cross, too.

"I'm so sorry," Quill said as she approached them.

"It's nothing to do with us," Collier snapped. "We hardly know the man."

"It is to do with us," Mrs. Barbarossa insisted. "The police won't let us leave until this is cleared up."

"I'm calling our lawyer," Anson Fredericks said. "This is ridiculous." He put his arm around his wife, who shook it off.

"Can we at least stay here with you, Quill?" Mrs. Barbarossa's faded blue eyes were teary.

Quill glanced at Dina, who kept the schedules.

"I'll see what I can do," Dina said doubtfully. "Of course, Mr. Vanderhausen's room is free for the next guest, but your room, Mr. Collier, and your room, Mrs. Barbarossa, are completely booked up. We had a last-minute cancellation, so the Frederickses are all right, but unless Meg moves in with Quill and frees up that space, we're completely booked."

"I can stay at the academy," Meg said.

"I'll stay at the Marriott," Collier said.

243

"Although as far as I can see, the police have no right to keep us here."

"Quill, you must find a space for Mr. Collier *here*," Mrs. Barbarossa said tearfully. "We all have to stick together."

Quill struggled to find a tactful way to ask the question uppermost in her mind and couldn't think of any. "Why?" she said. "Why do you all have to stick together? What does WARP stand for?"

Meg found tact a convenience rather than a necessity of character, so she was more to the point: "Who are you people, anyway?"

"If we don't have to tell the police, we certainly don't have to tell you," Muriel Fredericks said. She turned and glared at her husband. "I have to get out of this lobby, Anson. Right now. Take me down to the beach."

"The beach is closed," Anson said. "Some DEC thing."

Muriel took a deep breath. Quill's first impulse was to put her fingers in her ears (which would have been a violation of the Innkeeper's Code of Honor: always take it on the chin), but instead she put her hand under Muriel's elbow. "We're going out to the Tavern Lounge, all of us. You're going to have a little coffee and some freshly squeezed juice and just . . . enjoy the day."

She ignored Meg's traitorous snicker. "Dina? Get Mike to take the suitcases back upstairs. Get housekeeping to tidy Meg's room for whoever's checking in next. Mr. Collier? The Inn van will take you to the Marriott as soon as we arrange your reservation."

She acknowledged Dina's impressed, "Yes, ma'am!" with a backward wave of her hand.

Quill walked into the kitchen after settling Mrs. Barbarossa and the Frederickses in the Tavern Lounge. Collier had shrugged off her offer of coffee and pastry and stamped outside for a walk. When she came in, Dina was seated with Elizabeth Chou and Bjarne Bjarnsen over cups of chai.

"Wretched Allergies Recovery Program?" Dina guessed. "Wonky Adults Recovery Program? Weird Aggravators? We were just trying to guess what the acronym means. You know, the WARP people. It has to be a recovery program because of the Serenity Prayer we found in the wastebasket in Mr. Collier's room, so the 'R' and the 'P' are easy."

Quill sat down in the rocking chair. "I don't know what it means, and I have no idea why they are so secretive about it." She thought a minute. "And I wouldn't be all that sure about the 'R' and the 'P.' Maybe it's Rack and Pillage."

"Do you think WARP has anything to do with the murders?" Elizabeth asked.

Quill stopped the forward motion of the rocker with her toe. "I don't know," she said. "How could it?"

"It is just another one of the groups on the fringe that come here," Bjarne said. Bjarne was a Finn with a Swedish name who spoke both of those languages fluently and English quite well. He was tall, with eyes the color of a glass of water. He'd come into Meg's kitchen many years before, as a graduate student from the Cornell School of Hotel Administration, and he'd never left. He was a very good chef.

"It's nice to see you back," Quill said. "How was your vacation?"

"Not as interesting as this," Bjarne said. "And there has been another murder, too." He shook his head. "Too many guns about, I fear."

"Except nobody was shot," Dina pointed out. "Up until now, at least. What about Wayward Asthmatics Recovery Program?"

"It would be better to Google it, I think," Bjarne said. "Rather than driving us all mad with your suppositions."

Dina clapped her hands together. "Why didn't I think of that?"

"Because maybe you were going to see to that to-do list I just gave you?" Quill said.

"Already done," Dina said. "Reserved a room at the Marriott for Mr. Collier, talked to housekeeping about Meg's room and moving Mrs. Barbarossa's stuff. I got Mike to haul luggage, too, and Quill, everyone is so impressed with your executive decision-making, I can't tell you."

Quill surveyed the members of her kitchen staff, looking for impressed faces. Bjarne was absorbed in the memo about specials Meg had left for him. Elizabeth was de-stemming the last of the blueberries. Devon and Mallory were busy cleaning dishes. "Yes, well. I'm off."

Dina gave her a salute and asked, "Where are you going? Are you here or not here?"

"That depends. Are we still getting calls about places for that darn dinner now that it's on again?"

"Yes. And I put all the names in my sun hat. I thought I'd let Bjarne pick them out."

Bjarne raised his eyebrows. "What is this?"

Elizabeth nudged him. "Say no!"

"She thinks you'll be getting people annoyed with you, Bjarne," Quill explained. "Tell you what, Dina. Let everybody know the main course is going to be goat."

"Goat!" Dina looked appalled. "We're serving goat?"

"Goat is very tasty," Bjarne said reprovingly. "You Americans have absurd prejudices. Tell them it is chevon, and everyone will want to come."

"Tell them it's goat," Quill said. "We only have a limited number of seats. So, yes, I'm here, Dina. I'll keep my cell phone on."

"Where are you going?"

"To the library. I'm hot after a clue."

"You have to turn your cell phone off in the library." Miriam wore large, blue-rimmed spectacles that should have given her an owlish, schoolmarmish look but somehow managed to look sensual. Quill turned her cell phone off and whispered, "Where are the computers?"

"You don't have to whisper. Just turn your cell phone . . ."

"I did. Can you show me the computers? Preferably the one Mrs. Owens used when she was last in."

Miriam led the way through the stacks of books to the rear of the small building that held the village library. Adela chaired the library board. Just as John Deere bulldozers were good at moving dirt, Adela was good at fund-raising. So the library was a pleasant, well-ordered place with good lighting, lots of books, and up-to-date computer equipment. It was early, just after nine; the place was almost deserted, except for old Mrs. Nickerson who came in every day to read the *Democrat & Chronicle.*

"Right there." Miriam pointed to the middle of three desktop computers lined up against the wall. "But if you're hoping to find out where she browsed, you're out of luck."

"I am? On my laptop, when you go online, there's a little directory to show what sites you've visited in the past. Mine keeps that until it gets to five hundred, and then it starts deleting the older ones."

"You aren't used to a publicly accessed system. Do you have one available for the guests?"

"It's in a corner in the lobby. Dina handles it."

Miriam had been a schoolteacher before she went to library school, and her voice became quite teacher-ly. "When you log on to a public system, it deletes all the information from that session."

"All of it?"

"All of it."

Quill pulled out one of the hard plastic

chairs for users and sat down. "Phooey."

"Phooey, indeed."

"There are very few leads in this case, you know. Useful to me and Meg, I mean. I'm sure there's tons of scene-of-the-crime evidence, not to mention all the state and federal records that give the police and licensed private detectives background material not available to us. What we do is outside that system."

"That makes *some* sense," Miriam said, leaving Quill with the impression that she still thought Sarah Quilliam, snoop, was a bit of girlish foolishness. "Why would Mrs. Owens's website searches have anything to do with LeVasque's death?"

"I was thinking more along the lines of having something to do with *her* death."

Miriam stiffened in shock. "What? There's another body?"

"Oh, dear. Yes. She was killed last night, I guess."

"Where? How?"

"At the base of the statue in Peterson Park."

"*That* thing." (The statue of General C. C. Hemlock, on horseback, was quite dramatically awful.) "Are the killings linked? Was it the same MO as LeVasque's murder?"

Quill didn't point out that Miriam seemed to have abandoned her genial contempt for amateur detection. She did answer the question. "Doreen was a little foggy on that. She was hit with something, first, I think. Then she was stabbed. Sheriff Kiddermeister took Mr. Vanderhausen off for questioning this morning. Apparently his bowie knife was found lying near the body."

"So he didn't do it," Miriam said with satisfaction. "The most obvious suspect is always innocent. She sat down at one of the computers and began inputting. "What's Mrs. Owens's first name?"

"Nobody knows." Quill leaned over her and stared at the screen. "What are you doing?"

Miriam looked around, rather furtively. The only person Quill could see was Mrs. Nickerson, who was doing the newspaper crossword puzzle. "If you say a *word* about this to anyone, I'll put you at the bottom of the list for the next Louise Penny book."

"Okay. My lips are sealed."

Miriam clicked away for a few moments, then got up from the chair and pushed Quill into it. "Look."

Quill gasped. Miriam rapped her on the head with her knuckles. "Quiet!"

"Miriam, this is the preliminary sheriff's

report!" Quill looked up at her. "You hacked into the sheriff's files? How did you *do* that?"

"It helps if you sleep with the local judge, and that he's a very sound sleeper and keeps passwords in his wallet."

Miriam looked smug. Quill was appalled. But not too appalled to read the report on Mrs. Owens's death.

"Her first name is Verena," Quill said. "And she was robbed. Her purse was emptied, her cell phone smashed. And, oh, dear. She was hit on the head. The EMT at the scene thinks it didn't kill her, but that having her throat cut did. *Ugh!*" Quill pulled away from the screen.

"Sissy." Miriam shoved her aside. "Now let's look at the arrest report." Her fingers tapped at the keys. "I thought you said his name was Vanderhausen."

"That's how he's registered. And that's what his Centurion card said."

"He had an American Express Centurion card?"

"Yep. All of them did, as a matter of fact."

"A guy with a Centurion card mugs a middle-aged cook in the park for what? A hundred bucks? Tops? That doesn't make any sense."

"You said his name wasn't really Vanderhausen. Maybe the real Mr. Vanderhausen is loaded."

"He'd have to be, to have a Centurion card. The credit card companies only give those out to the top one per cent of our richest citizens, bastards that they are."

Since Quill wasn't sure whether Miriam referred to the credit card companies or the rich, she let it go. "What is Vanderhausen's real name?"

Miriam sat back and looked at her fingers in admiration. Then she bent over the keyboard and started clicking away again. "Bobby Ray Steinmetz. And he's a known felon. There were clear fingerprints on the knife, and forensics got a match just like that."

"Armed robbery," Quill said. "I do know about that."

"Holy crow!" Miriam sat back, her eyebrows raised. "Look at this!"

Quill bent forward to read the screen. A story headline from *USA Today* shouted: "Convicted Felon Wins Lottery!"

Bobby Ray Steinmetz had won fifty million dollars.

Miriam stared at her. "In case you're wondering, the look you see on my face is one of wild surmise."

Quill thought hard for a minute. "Why

would someone who'd just won all that money want to mug Mrs. Owens? You're right. It doesn't make sense. Shove aside a minute, Miriam. I want to try something."

"No."

"No, I can't try something?"

"No, let me do it." She smiled. She had dimples, and she looked quite raffish. "This is a lot more fun than cataloguing books."

"Okay. Try the acronym WARP."

"You still don't know what that group is all about?"

"They wouldn't even tell the sheriff. But I've just had a chilling thought."

Miriam tsk-tsked. "Cliché, cliché." Then, chattily, as she bent once again to the keyboard, "Have you noticed that everyone's calling Davy 'sheriff' now? He's really grown into the job. Howie always said he would."

"Myles, too."

"Boo-hiss," Miriam said as the screen filled up with the black and blue listings. "All I'm getting is *Star Trek* stuff. Your WARPs are a no-go."

Quill concentrated. "Try Arnold Henry Vanderhausen."

Miriam typed in the name. The search took longer than usual, and when the name finally came up, Quill felt a thud of excitement.

"He's a lottery winner, too," Miriam said. "A dead lottery winner. He won three hundred million dollars in the Florida lottery in 1996 and died six months later in a spa whirlpool with two Brazilian models."

"Try this pair of names: Muriel and Anson Fredericks."

This search took as long as the first.

Quill and Miriam stared at the screen and then at each other.

"Now, William Knight Collier."

"And Mrs. Valerie Barbarossa."

The search was faster this time, and the two of them read the results in silence. "All of them," Quill said finally. "All of them named after dead lottery winners. Miriam. They all registered under false names. All those people at my Inn are crooks!"

"Oh, my God." Miriam breathed. "It's a bloody gang!"

16

Behind every great chef is a superior staff. Do not make the mistake of settling for second best. But they must always remember who is in charge.

— *The Master at Work,*
starring Bernard LeVasque,
Episode 3

Quill's first panicked thought was Jack. Her precious baby lodged in the same place as a bunch of felons. It didn't bear thinking of. She had to get them out. And she had to get them out now. She gunned her Honda up the hill, hoping that every single traffic patrolperson in Hemlock Falls was too busy investigating Bobby Ray Steinmetz to pay attention to speeders. She parked in the traffic circle and raced in the front door.

"You're back," Dina said in welcome. She stood up behind the desk at the sight of

Quill's face. "Is anything wrong? Are you okay?"

Quill battled to remain calm. One thing was certain; she couldn't let anybody see her this upset. "Everything's fine," she said carelessly. "But I had a thought. Maybe we should move all the WARP people to the Marriott. Could you book them rooms, please? And then have Mike take them over in the van? And could you have them all out by noon?" Doreen had taken Jack to the Y for a morning playdate. They would be back by noon.

"Noon is when Jack and Doreen come back," Dina said with uncanny prescience.

"Is it?" Quill said lightly. Then, urgently, "Can you take care of this please? Right now?"

"Sure! I'll just tell Mrs. Barbarossa that we weren't able to rearrange the bookings after all. I'll tell the Fredrickses that the annual room fumigation is scheduled for this afternoon and she'll scream 'eww' and bolt out of here like a rabbit. No sweat."

"Thank you." Quill sat down on the couch in front of the little stone fireplace and took several deep breaths. Then she hit the speed dial on her cell and called Doreen.

"What?" Doreen demanded when she answered.

"Just called to see how things are going." In the background, Quill heard the shrieking of little kids. "Is that Jack I hear?"

Doreen snorted. "I bring 'em up better than that. He knows better than to hit another kid with a toy truck. What you're hearing is Francie Neidermier's grandson. Kid's a brat. Jack's just about to go down the kiddie slide. He's waitin' his turn, like a good boy."

A piercing howl seemed to indicate some kind of resolution to the battle of the toy truck.

"What's up?" Doreen demanded.

"Not a thing," Quill said hastily. "When you bring Jack back for his nap, you'll be sure to stay with him, won't you?"

"I always do." Doreen was as patient with Quill as she was with Jack, which was a very good thing. "That all you called for?"

"That's all."

Doreen clicked off. She wasn't one to stand on ceremony.

Dina spoke up. "Whatever's upsetting you is going to upset those WARP people if they run into you. Maybe you could take a walk while I get this settled."

"No. I'll be at the academy. There's something I have to find out on Mrs. Owens's own computer. Plus, I need to talk to Meg.

And, Dina? Call me when those people are out of here."

"No problem." Dina picked up the phone. "I'm on it." She stopped, her finger poised over the speed dial. "Anything else? Would you like me to call somebody? Can I get you a cup of tea?"

"Not a thing." Quill forced herself to get up and move. She sped back through town, keeping a wary eye out for traffic patrol, and made the trip to the academy in five minutes flat.

A black-and-white patrol car was parked at the academy annex. A dark blue Crown Victoria sat next to it. Chances were high that the police were going through Verena Owens's apartment. And chances were slim to none that they were going to let a civilian like Quill rummage through Verena's computer.

Quill debated with herself, then parked the Honda in the main lot. She had to let Davy know right away about the unmasking of the WARP group. Miriam was sworn to secrecy, but Quill was willing to bet her vow would last until the second glass of Chardonnay at the Croh Bar.

As expected, she was barred from going any farther than the annex foyer. She told the patrolman at the door there was an urgent message for the sheriff. She waited impatiently for several minutes. Davy finally emerged from the hallway that led to Mrs. Owens's apartment.

"You look tired," she said, with sudden concern.

He rubbed his hand over his unshaven chin. "I'm beat. I don't mean to put you off, Quill, but can't this wait?"

"I think it might be important."

"Okay. Spill it."

"None of the people in the WARP group are who they say they are."

"What do you mean?"

Quill bit her lip. Damn it all. This was going to be tricky. She couldn't reveal how Miriam hacked into the police computers. And — unworthy as it was — she was banking on whom she was married to to keep her out of trouble. "I think that Valerie Barbarossa, William Knight Collier, and Anson and Muriel Fredericks are all assumed names."

"Is that a fact?" Davy unwrapped a piece of gum, stuck it in his mouth, and chewed it. He appeared to be thinking something over. Quill was pretty sure she knew what it was: somehow, Myles McHale's wife had gotten hold of information known only to the police — the real name of the chief suspect in a nasty case of murder. He wanted to know how. If he knew how, he might have to arrest her. It was okay to arrest Sarah Quilliam. As a matter of fact, right about now he'd enjoy it. It was very not okay to arrest Myles McHale's wife.

The solidarity that characterizes police forces the world over won out. Davy said, "How do you figure that?"

"It's because they won't tell us what WARP stands for. I mean, here you've arrested this guy with a record — and he's an accepted member of a group that includes a banker, a stockbroker, and a little old lady with grandchildren in the dairy business. It didn't make sense. So I Googled WARP . . ."

"*Star Trek* stuff," Davy said.

"Exactly. So I Googled their names."

Davy's expression relaxed a little. "Yeah? That was pretty smart. You get something out of that?"

"Everybody's dead. I mean, the names are all of people who're dead. Lottery winners, as a matter of fact, but my guess is that was just a handy way to find useful aliases. I mean Vanderhausen, or rather Bobby Ray Steinmetz actually won one. I think that's where they got the idea. More than that, I think it's a gang. I thought you ought to know."

"What kind of gang?"

"I don't know! Maybe they make a habit of robbing live lottery winners. Maybe they plan to rip off the Hemlock Falls First National Bank. What I do know is that they're unbelievably secretive. Whatever they're planning, I'll bet they've done it before."

Davy nodded agreement. "Dina says they spend money like drunken Indians."

"Dina would never say that. I mean, yes, they spend a lot and in kind of careless ways. But not like . . ."

A smile lightened his eyes. "Nope, and she'd clock me a good one if she knew I'd said it that way, too. So don't blow me in, okay?"

"Okay. Anyhow, as soon as I found out, I came to tell you. I thought you ought to know."

"Thanks. I'll see about it."

"I don't suppose you'll tell me when you find out?"

"Don't push it, Quill."

"I wouldn't," she said apologetically. "It's just that with Jack there . . . oh! And there's one more thing. I moved them all to the Marriott."

"Good. We'll know where to find them."

"What are you going to do now?"

"Now, look, Quill . . ."

"The reason I asked, is because there might be some clues to Mrs. Owens's activities before she died on her computer."

"She doesn't have a computer." He chewed his gum twice and then added, "We didn't find one. You know anything about her computer?"

"Not really," she said cautiously. "But I heard."

"Heard what? From who? And how?"

She raised her hands in defeat. "Sorry. You're right. I'll be up at the kitchens if you need me."

Davy smiled at her. "If I tell you don't hold your breath, will you get mad?"

There was a back entrance to the restaurant kitchen. Quill was pretty sure she'd find Meg there, so she took the path that circumnavigated the building. Pietro Giancava stood in the little landscaped area just outside the kitchen itself, smoking a cigarette. He pinched it out as Quill came up and tossed it into a holly bush. "She is inside, your sister, rearranging all. I am not happy."

"The menu, you mean?"

"Of course, the menu. What else?"

Quill smiled at him. Cranky chefs were a

familiar problem. "You, yourself, Pietro, would want to present your own work at a dinner like the one tomorrow night and not someone else's."

He smoothed his thick black hair with both hands. "I am, of course, a better chef than it may appear from my current station in life. Maitre Quilliam has seen that I have a . . . how would you put it . . . a genius with sauces. So yes. Unlike that rascal LeVasque, she has stated openly that I am to create my sauce Milanese for the chevon. However!" He paused, opened the door for her, and followed her inside. "We have not yet reached an agreement on the wines. She is insisting on using *les vins du pays.* There is not one acceptable red in the whole of this area. You must speak to her. The Rieslings?" He threw his hands in the air. "I have given up. I will use the Rieslings."

Meg stood in the center of the gorgeous kitchen, frowning over a clipboard. She looked up as Quill and Pietro came in. "Hey, sis," she said absently. "And I heard that about the reds, Pietro." She looked around. "Anybody have a paper bag?"

Raleigh Brewster was at a huge ash prep table, chopping green peppers with furious abandon. "There's a stack in the commodities room."

"The commodities room," Meg repeated. "This place doesn't have a mere pantry. It's got a commodities room. Could you get one for me, please, Raleigh? And give it to Pietro." She tucked the clipboard under her arm and beamed at her sister. "Isn't this place gorgeous?"

Quill had to agree. The floor — although it was covered in most places by thick rubber matting — was made of beautifully marled cork, easy on the feet and wonderful to the eye. The cupboards were from Smallbone, in the Baroque style, with fluted pillars supporting the prep tables. The huge room had windows on three sides, so that the place was filled with light.

"What am I to do with this paper bag?" Pietro scowled.

"You are to put it over your head and taste three Finger Lakes Pinot Noirs and three French Pinot Noirs. If you tell the difference between them I will personally give you ten thousand dollars. Of course, if you can't, you will have to give me ten thousand dollars."

"Still want the paper bag?" Raleigh asked.

Pietro tossed his head. "How much is ten thousand dollars in euros?"

A ripple of laughter went through the kitchen. Pietro grinned. "Okay. I give it to you. We will use the Keuka Spring red with the chevon, okay? It is tolerable."

"It's more than tolerable. It's fabulous."

Quill touched her sister on the arm. "Can I talk to you a minute?"

"Sure. LeVasque has this fabulous office. It's right over here."

The office was at the front of the kitchen, right off the big glass doors that led in from the lobby. Meg stopped at each of the workstations on the way, testing a reduction, inspecting the texture of a country pâté, suggesting an adjustment to a sorbet mixture of late raspberries. Quill controlled her impatience with an effort. Just before they went into the late LeVasque's office, she turned and surveyed the kitchen. "We're using almost all apprentices," she said to Quill in an undertone, "but it's working out pretty well. I sure could use Clare, though. It takes years to learn good pastry, and even then, she's got a gift. Poor Mrs. Owens doesn't seem to be much of a loss, though. Raleigh volunteered to supervise the compotes and I think it's going to work out just fine."

Quill put her hand on her arm. "We need to talk about the murders."

"Quill! I've got a huge dinner in less than thirty-six hours!"

"And we need to get Clare out of jail!"

"Oh. Right." Meg shoved the office door open.

The place was splendidly furnished. Coffee-colored area rugs covered the cherry floor. Tall filing cabinets of the same wood stood at each end of a sideboard with a sink and under-counter refrigerator. A long cherry conference table surrounded by executive chairs was under a bay window. The chairs were upholstered in fine beige leather.

This side of the academy building faced Peterson Park and the window took full advantage of the view. The statue of General Hemlock was partly visible through a small grove of maple trees. Quill noted there was only one entrance to the office: the big glass door they had come through.

Meg dropped her clipboard on LeVasque's big cherry desk. "Okay. Shoot. What's up?"

Quill took a seat in the chair next to the desk. "Every single member of WARP signed in with us under the name of a dead lottery winner."

Meg's mouth opened and closed. Then she said, "Why?"

"I have no idea why."

"What does this have to do with LeVasque's death?"

"I can't imagine."

"Does it have anything to do with Mrs. Owens's death?"

"I don't know." Quill picked up Meg's clipboard, unsnapped the top, and began to neaten the pages up. "I'll tell you what I think, though. Whoever killed Mrs. Owens wants us to think that. I mean, why else set up Bobby Ray Steinmetz for it?"

"Bobby who?"

"That's Vanderhausen's real name. But he doesn't have any sort of obvious motive. He won some humongous amount in the Florida Lottery and he didn't need to rob anyone, that's for sure. And guess how I found out his real name?"

"Davy told you?"

Quill made a face. "Davy's behaving like . . . well . . . like a sheriff. And you're not going to believe this!" She re-clipped the tidy stack of pages to the clipboard and told her about Miriam.

"Holy crow." Meg sat down at LeVasque's desk. "So now what?"

"Now I take a look at Bonne Goutè's personnel files." She looked around the office. "Unless you've got them already ready? How's your end of the investigation going?"

"I've been menu planning! I can't just pull a menu for thirty out of my ear. Not to mention trying to get some kind of performance out of a bunch of wet-behind-the-ears apprentices." Meg's face was pink and cross.

Quill couldn't check the color of her sister's socks; it was summer and she wore clogs in the kitchen. You could calculate Meg's temper most of the year by her sock selection. It just wasn't possible in summer. "Don't worry about it. Just tell me where to find the files, and I'll get them myself." She patted the monitor of the desktop computer in LeVasque's desk. "Are they in here?"

"Probably not. My guess is they're in that big filing cabinet." Meg got up, went to the elegant cabinet in the corner, and pulled out the middle drawer. She took a clutch of keys from her apron pocket, sorted through them, and fitted the smallest into the drawer lock. She rummaged a bit and said, "Here." She handed Quill a thick stack of manila folders. "Can I go back to work now? I promise I'm keeping my ears open for any stray confessions that might come up over the goat carcass."

Quill hefted the stack of files in one hand. "I can't walk out of here with these."

"You can put them in this." Meg knelt on the floor and stuck her head under the desk. "You are not going to believe it. We should

think about something like this for the Inn."
Then she snorted. "Not!" She emerged with
a handsome canvas tote. One side was lettered with the culinary academy logo. The
other had a full color reproduction of
LeVasque's face. "If Harvey Bozzel's seen
this, the town's in trouble," Meg predicted
darkly. "There'll be totes shrieking *mayor*
on one side with Elmer's smiling face on
the other. Everybody will want one. We'll
walk down Main Street and it will look like
everybody's carrying their heads." She
hummed a line from a rowdy ballad about
Anne Boleyn: *"With their heads tucked underneath their arms."*

"This place is making you giddy." Quill
shoved the files into the tote. "It's a start.
I'll go through these tonight. And somehow,
I've got to get into Mrs. Owens's personal
computer. Miriam says she spent a lot of
time on the Internet at the library before
she bought her own PC. There might be
something there. It'd be really great if I
could get in to talk to Bobby Ray Steinmetz,
too, but in the mood Davy's in, there's not
much hope. On the other hand, if the
interview notes go into the police case file,
there's always good old Miriam."

"What are you two doing in here!" Madame had entered so quietly, neither Meg

nor Quill had heard her approach. The widow was in black. Black skirt, black blouse, and black lace-up shoes. A black headband held back her iron gray hair. Quill jumped. Meg, possessed of more sangfroid than was good for her character, waved the clipboard at her. "I was looking for a copy of Chef LeVasque's book, *Brilliance in the Kitchen.* Thought I'd check out some of his recipes."

"There are copies available in the gift shop." Madame glowered and nodded sharply at the tote Quill carried. "What is that?"

"Recipes," Meg said. "Recipes, recipes."

"Madame?" Raleigh Brewster stuck her head in the door. "Two guys in suits are here to see you."

"Three-piece suits?" Meg bustled forward and took Madame's arm. Behind her back, she gestured energetically at Quill, who tucked the tote out of sight under her feet. "Must be lawyers. Did you call for your lawyers?"

"His lawyers." Madame looked more sour than ever.

Meg raised her eyebrows. "You have separate lawyers?"

Madame worked her thin lips. "LeVasque was a secretive son of a bitch."

Raleigh rapped the paneled wall with her knuckles. "Where do you want me to put the men in suits, Madame?" She added testily, "I'm in the middle of a pistou."

"What about the reception office?" Meg suggested. "Or the tasting room? I can send in some brioche and maybe some fruit? I bet they'd like that."

"Send them in here." Madame walked to the conference table in her flat-footed way and sat at the head of the table. Raleigh backed away from the office door and made a "come in" gesture.

Two men walked in, both in three-piece pin-striped suits. The older one was balding, with wire-rimmed glasses and a slight paunch. The younger one was thin, with the wiry build of a runner. He'd shaved his head. Quill always wondered about men who shaved their heads. She had to fight the impulse to polish their skulls with the first available tissue.

"Eddie Barstow," the older one said, "of Barstow and Phipps. And this is David Phipps." He smiled at Meg. "And you," he said genially, "must be Margaret Quilliam. Congratulations on inheriting the academy. From what Dave and I have seen so far, it's a wonderful place."

17

∼Betty Hall's Reuben Sandwich∼

1/2 pound finest corned beef
1/4 cup Silver Floss sauerkraut
1-ounce slice very nutty Swiss cheese
2 slices finest pumpernickel bread, cut thick
4 ounces sweet creamery butter

Brush all sides of bread with melted fresh creamery butter. Whisk the corned beef through the melted butter and sauté quickly. Place both pieces of pumpernickel on a plate. Add one tablespoon Betty's Thousand Island dressing* to each slice. Heap with corned beef. Add sauerkraut and Swiss cheese. Broil sandwich quickly. Serve with dill pickle and deep-fried potato chips.

*Not available to the public. Ever.

Two hours later, Meg was still pale with

shock and excitement. Quill wasn't feeling too settled herself. The two of them sat at the Croh Bar, in the booth farthest from the front. The Croh Bar was nice, neutral territory, and the chances of running into anyone from either the Inn or the academy were slim. Marge had bought it from Norm Pasquale when he'd retired to Florida ten years ago. It was a popular place, and other than replacing the beat-up, old indoor-outdoor carpeting with new, in exactly the same pattern, she had wisely left the interior alone. The battered wood bar was up front. Booths with red vinyl seats lined both walls. A clutter of small round tables ran down the middle. It was dark, since the row of windows facing Main Street always had the dusty green shades drawn. It had a pleasantly musty smell of stale beer, moldy carpet, and the antiseptic Betty Hall used to keep the kitchen clean. It was just before noon, and the place was starting to fill up. Meg always said Betty Hall was the best short-order cook in the east, and the citizens of Hemlock Falls agreed with her.

Quill picked up her glass of iced tea and set it down again. "Well," she said.

"I can't believe it." Meg ran her hands through her hair. Quill figured this was the one-hundredth time Meg had said she couldn't believe it, and the two-hundredth time she'd run her hands through her hair.

"I must look awful." Meg never carried a purse. Quill rummaged in her own and pulled out a small mirror and a comb. Meg stared into the mirror and handed it back. "I do look awful. Quill, what are we going to do?"

"What we just did." Quill was in the seat that faced the front of the bar and the entrance to the street. She saw Marge come in and waved at her.

"There you are." Marge stumped up and settled herself next to Meg. "You come in for lunch?" She wriggled her eyebrows at them. Marge always dressed in chinos, no matter what the weather, but she varied her tops. Today she wore a cotton blouse patterned with tiny little cows.

"You heard," Meg said hollowly.

"You need a sandwich," Marge said. Then, without moving, she yelled, "Bets!"

Betty Hall stuck her head out of the kitchen.

"Three Reubens."

"Got it!"

"I don't think I can eat anything," Meg said. "Not just yet."

"I heard they had to sedate that there Madame," Marge said. "That true?"

275

"Not exactly," Quill hesitated.

"She sure was mad," Meg said with awe. "She stood up and yelled. Just yelled. Like: 'Aaahhhh!' "

"Yeah? She pass out then, or what?"

"Unfortunately, no," Quill said. "And then she picked up that big purse she carries and belted Barstow over the head with it. Or maybe it was Phipps. The bald one."

"Phipps," Meg said. "I remember because I wanted to polish his head when he walked in."

"You, too?" Quill said. "Hm."

Marge drummed her fingers on the Formica tabletop.

Quill sighed and continued, "And Phipps started to bleed — you know, Marge, one of the purposes of hair is to protect you from getting belted over the head. It's just dumb to shave it all off. You never know when you're going to get belted with something."

"So somebody called the EMTs," Marge interrupted. "Was it because of this Phipps bleeding all over?"

"Raleigh Brewster did that. Made the emergency call. Head wounds do bleed a lot, and Mr. Phipps was running around the kitchen with Mrs. LeVasque running after him."

"Yelling, 'Bastard! Bastard!' " Meg put in.

"We weren't sure whether she meant Phipps or her dead husband."

"And it got into the pistou," Quill said. "Some blood."

"So the pistou is ruined," Meg said with a gusty sigh.

Betty Hall arrived with the sandwiches and put the plates down. She was thin, with black hair, and in all the years Quill had known her, she'd spoken almost nothing.

Meg poked at the Reuben, which smelled wonderful and oozed Swiss cheese in all the right places. "This looks perfect, Betty. And you're using homemade sauerkraut. Impressive."

Betty smiled and went away.

"Eat it," Marge ordered. "And then maybe you'll start to make some sense. You're both hysterical."

Quill took an indignant bite of her sandwich. "We aren't hysterical. It's been a rough morning."

Marge took a generous bite of her own. "So then what?"

Meg grinned. It was a tentative, weak grin, but Quill was relieved to see that her sister was recovering a little. Meg waved half of the Reuben in the air and said, "Madame kept on bashing at Phipps until Jim Chen and Pietro threatened to sit on her. They got her off Phipps and sat her down. And then Davy came, with the EMTs, and they took Phipps off. And Barstow disappeared into the office with Davy and Madame.

"But you know, I don't think it was unexpected. Not that LeVasque had tried to leave the academy to me, but that he didn't leave it to her."

"Tried to?" Marge said alertly.

"We couldn't accept it, of course," Quill said quietly.

"You said *no?!*" Marge roared.

"Of course we said no." Meg sat up a little straighter. "It's outrageous, Marge. That place should go to his wife. They've been married for forty-two years! This was just another one of LeVasque's spiteful jokes."

Marge's shrewd gray eyes darted from one sister to the other.

"We were tempted, of course," Quill said. "To be honest."

"She means me," Meg said in a small voice. "Marge — have you seen those kitchens? For just a moment, there . . ."

Marge groaned. "You walked away from a multimillion-dollar property for some half-assed principle? You didn't let her sign anything, did you, Quill?"

"There was too much of a ruckus to do anything but scoot out of there. I pulled

Barstow aside and told him we'd have Howie give him a call, because we absolutely could not accept this, under any circumstances."

"And what'd he say? Maybe you and Meg can't give it back."

"He said, 'Fine.' And was I sure I wanted to do this. And I said I was never surer of anything in my life."

Marge thumped the table in disgust. "You know what I ought to do? I ought to charge you double for lunch. How do you like that for a principle?"

"I'll tell you what I'd like. I'd like to figure out who killed LeVasque so we can get Clare out of jail and back into the kitchen. Meg's still got a dinner for thirty tomorrow night."

"So you two are still in the detecting business, huh? Figured as much."

"Clare's in jail," Meg said. "And she didn't do it. Quill and I are going to get her out."

"By finding out who killed the grouchy gourmet?" Marge snorted. But it was an affectionate snort.

"And Mrs. Owens," Quill said. "The two murders are connected, Marge, they have to be."

"Try this one on," Marge suggested.

"LeVasque knows his wife's likely to bump him off so he leaves the place to you."

"That crossed my mind," Quill admitted. "But then, he would have told her, wouldn't he? That he was leaving it to Meg?"

"Maybe he did."

Quill shook her head. "It wouldn't have been such a shock, if he had."

"She might have read you two right. Knew that chances were pretty good you'd . . ." Marge stopped, apparently unable to actually say aloud that Meg had given up a multimillion-dollar gift. "Anyways, I know this for a fact. She could have taken you to court to get the thing back. That way, everybody's miserable except the lawyers. That kind of trick was right up LeVasque's alley."

"Whatever his reason, it makes one thing pretty clear to me." Quill counted out the bills for their lunch, then collected her purse and the tote with the Bonne Goutè personnel files and got out of the booth.

Marge looked up at her.

"Madame just became the number one suspect in her husband's murder. Meg? Do you want a ride anywhere? I'm going to see if I can track Howie down."

"I'd better get back up to the school. You're right. I've still got the dinner tomorrow night. Unless you think the Chamber would be willing to cancel, Marge? At the moment, I can guarantee a refund."

"You're kidding me, right? You couldn't keep 'em away with a stick." She gave Meg's arm a friendly thump. "I'll run her back up there, Quill. And then if you don't mind, I'm going to do a little poking around myself. Into the financial affairs of that late loony tune, Bernard LeVasque. I'd like to see just how much money you two gave away to that old biddy of a widow."

18

Renounce: to announce one's abandon-
ment or the ownership of; to give up,
abandon, or formally resign something
possessed.

— Webster's Third New
International Dictionary

Howie Murchison's law offices were just off
Main, on a quiet street with brick houses
and a bicycle shop. Howie's great-
grandfather Howard Charles Murchison,
had started the family tradition of going into
law, and he practiced from the same house
Howie lived in now. It was a big place, a
center-entrance Georgian with three floors
and a large backyard. Howie's offices took
up most of the first floor. The dining room
and the kitchen were on the right. The offices were on the left. Quill doubted that
the reception area, the small law library,
and Howie's office itself had ever been a

parlor or living room. Those were on the second floor, where Howie's bedroom was located.

The front door was always open. Quill walked into the black-and-white-tiled foyer, tapped at the paneled door labeled OFFICE and stuck her head inside. Nobody was at the secretary's desk, but she could see Howie's own office door was open, and she could see him at his computer.

"Hello?" Quill called out.

The door to the library opened and Justin Martinez looked out at her. "Hey, Quill!"

"Hey, Justin."

Hearing her voice, Howie got up and came out to join them. He indicated a worn leather couch with a sweep of his hand. "Glad to see you. Have a seat. I understand there was quite a commotion at the academy this morning."

Quill couldn't help but glance at the secretary's empty chair. Trish Peterson had been Howie's secretary for years, and she was connected to more people in Hemlock Falls than old Harland himself, which was saying something.

Howie chuckled. "No, it wasn't Trish. I got a call from Ed Barstow."

"Is Mr. Phipps okay?"

Howie shrugged. "As far as I know. It

wasn't much of a clunk on the head, according to Barstow. No concussion, but he needed a stitch or two."

Quill sat on the edge of the couch. "So you know why I'm here?"

"You want Justin to order a writ to forfeit any claim on the legacy of the late, and apparently unlamented, LeVasque." Howie wedged himself onto a corner of the secretary's desk. He wore rumpled gray trousers, a rumpled blue shirt, and his striped tie was askew. Quill found his whole demeanor extremely reassuring.

"So it's possible to do it? Marge thought that maybe we were stuck with it."

"Of course it's possible. You can't be forced to accept an inheritance if you don't want to." He looked at her over his half-glasses. They were tortoiseshell and were a useful adjunct to his sterner pronouncements from the bench. "The process is called Renunciation."

Quill had a quick vision of Christians sprawled among the lions in the arenas of ancient Rome "And what will happen to the property?"

"It devolves to the next heirs, by law."

"Which would be Mrs. LeVasque."

"Presumably. But you never know. LeVasque might have named someone else, on the chance that you two'd refuse it."

"Barstow's getting a copy of the will to us," Justin said. "I'll take a look at it and we'll get the Renunciation going right away. If you two are sure that's what you want to do."

"Couldn't be surer," Quill said simply. "Thank you both. But what happens until *that* happens? I mean, who's in charge over there? Who pays the salaries and sees that things are kept up?"

"The court can appoint a guardian," Justin said. "It'd be better if you and Mrs. LeVasque could come to some informal agreement." Quill's hand went to her head involuntarily at this suggestion. "I'm assuming that she signs the payroll checks. She was the manager of the place, wasn't she? Let's hope she's willing to keep things rolling along until the dust settles."

"She doesn't seem to be the sort of person to let the roof fall in, no. But it'd be better, maybe, if one of you two talked it over with her."

"I'll have a chat with Barstow," Justin said. "I have to go through her counsel."

"That'll take some time," Quill muttered. "Darn. Look. I'll go on up and talk to her myself. There's just one more thing."

"Clarissa Sparrow?" Justin said. "We're

working on it."

"Can I see her, do you think?"

"She's going to be moved today, to Five Points."

The correctional facility was out on Route 96, near the little town of Covert. It wasn't a long drive, but it would take time. And time was one thing she was short of. Quill rubbed her forehead. She was getting a headache.

"You can see her there, Quill. You know that the station here doesn't have the facilities to keep a prisoner for longer than twenty-four hours."

"Are they moving Mr. Steinmetz, too?"

"I don't know. He's got a high-priced lawyer coming in from Manhattan, that I do know. But you don't need to be worried about him, do you?"

"I was hoping to talk to him. Do you think he'd see me?"

Howie frowned a little. "I thought Quilliam and Quilliam had suspended operations," he said. "Myles . . ."

"Myles is fully aware of everything," Quill said tartly.

"Quilliam and Quilliam?" Justin looked puzzled. "Isn't the Inn incorporated under something else?"

"Quill and Meg's detective agency operates on an ad hoc basis," Howie said drily.

"Never mind," Quill said brightly. She'd just remembered Miriam. Of course. The case notes would be written up by now. They could move old Bobby Ray to Timbuktu, as long as it was online, and she'd still be able to get his story. Quill smiled sunnily at both men. "Thank you, Howie. I feel so safe knowin' you big, strong men are lookin' out for me."

Justin looked alarmed. Howie looked suspicious. Quill waved as charmingly as she could and went to tackle Madame.

She drove back to the academy feeling a lot of sympathy for gerbils, stuck on a little wheel hour after hour. She'd spent more time at the academy in the past few days than she had in her own bed.

The parking lot was almost empty. The place looked quiet and serene in the sunlight. The first faint tinge of fall colors had touched the maples out front. A tour bus pulled away from the circular drive as she parked, full of chattering tourists.

She decided against going into the building by way of the kitchen. Meg would have her hands full getting the staff to focus on tomorrow night's dinner. She doubted that Mrs. LeVasque would be there. She wouldn't want to interfere with what was perhaps the final income-earning event. If the woman hadn't decided to run away for good — and Quill wouldn't blame her if she had — she'd most probably be in LeVasque's office, standing guard over the accounts.

She was right. The scared-looking receptionist at the front desk was clearly loath to call her, so Quill simply said, "I'll let her know I'm here myself, shall I?"

"Thanks!" The girl, who was young, and not, Quill recalled, from Hemlock Falls, chewed nervously at her lower lip. "Things have been a little upset here."

"But you got that tour bus through, I see?"

"Last one of the day, thank goodness." She took a deep breath. "I guess I could call Madame, if you'd like."

"No problem. Really. I know the way."

Quill walked through the tasting room, which was littered with crumpled napkins, bits of cracker, and used wineglasses. She pushed through the doors to the back; the kitchen was down a short hall, and she glimpsed a lot of flurry. But it was normal flurry; the clink of pans and the chatter of people working together may have been a little more self-conscious than usual, but Meg clearly had things well in hand.

Quill tapped at the office door and went

in. Madame sat at the conference table, her head bent over a stack of papers, staring at her hands. She raised her head as Quill came in.

"You," she said.

"It's me. I thought maybe we could talk a bit?"

"All right."

Quill settled herself at the opposite end of the table.

"Madame," she began.

"You can call me Dorothy," she said unexpectedly. "I'm getting pretty tired of this Madame stuff." She sat back and looked out the window. The sunlight wasn't kind to her face. Years of angry living had left their mark in the furrows from her nose to her mouth. The skin under her eyes was puckered and yellowish from fatigue. But her eyes were sharp and hard, and her posture erect. Quill fought the impulse to grab her charcoal pencil and start to sketch. She could see this woman challenging the rush of winter water over the falls in the gorge.

"You meant what you said about giving up the academy?" Her voice was suspicious, disbelieving.

"Yes. I've just come from our lawyer's office and asked him to start the paperwork.

The process is called Renunciation and it means we don't want it." Quill winced at herself. "I didn't mean that the way it sounded. It's a wonderful place. It has everything my sister's ever dreamed of and anyone who loves food and wine and the whole business of delighting guests would want it. But it can never belong to us."

"It certainly won't," she snapped. "I'd fight you with everything I've got."

"There's no need. Truly."

"So. I hope your lawyer's quick about it."

"As quick as he can be," Quill promised. "I didn't come here to talk about that — well, I did, in a way, because I wanted to be sure that you were comfortable seeing to things here. We wouldn't want there to be any interruption in your services, either . . ." Quill trailed off. This uncompromising, suspicious woman was making it difficult. "Anyhow, I just came to say that things should continue just as they are."

"They will."

"And to ask you if you have any idea who killed your husband." Quill got this out in a rush.

"Police think it's that Clare Sparrow."

"I'm sure it isn't."

"She had a contract. She had to pay us a lot of money if she quit on us."

"She didn't quit. She was fired. And there's no employment contract in the world that would force a financial penalty under those circumstances. Not to be rude about it, Dorothy, but Clare was relieved to be out from your husband's thumb. Why kill him now? If she were going to kill him, why not before, when she thought she was indentured for the next God-knows-how-many years?"

A small, sour smile crossed Madame's face. "You've got a point there. So?" She shrugged. "He's dead. If Clare didn't do it, somebody did. And either the cops will find out or they won't. What's it to you?"

"I've got a good friend who's had a very bad time and she's headed for a worse one. It isn't fair. And justice . . . justice isn't all it's cracked up to be. So it means a lot to me."

"Fair enough. What do you want from me? You think I did it? What's more, if you think I did it, do you think I would tell you?"

"I wondered about that. But no, I don't think you did it."

Madame raised her eyebrows in mock appreciation.

"You needed him too much. He was the main attraction here. He was outrageous and rude, but he was the guiding genius behind this place, and you of all people wouldn't kill the goose with the golden egg. No matter how he treated you. It's just like Clare. If his behavior was going to drive you to murder, you would have done it long before you incurred all this."

They both looked out the window. The sun was low in the sky and the shadow cast by the academy spread over the fine green lawn.

"He had money on him," Madame said suddenly. "I figure whoever stuck him, robbed him. You want my opinion about who did it, it was one of them out there." She waved at the lawns. One of the gardeners was pushing a wheelbarrow along the graveled paths, picking up sticks and wayward plastic bags. "We try and do background checks on all our people, but it takes time and money."

"Just because someone's a gard . . ." Quill bit her lip. Meg had a T-shirt that read: *Help me! Help me! I'm talking and I can't shut up!* She'd meant to get one of her own. Instead, she said, "Was it a lot of money?"

"A fair bit. It was in fifties, or so it seemed to me. A wad about this thick." She held her finger and thumb apart about an inch."

"Where did it come from?"

"God knows. He liked his toys, Bernie

did. I let him have a personal account just to get him off my back." She said, without apparent irony, "Makes a better marriage that way. Anyhow, it wasn't on him when the police went over the body. Like I said, I want it back."

"But you didn't tell the police about it."

Madame smiled that sour smile. "I don't have to tell you about that, do I? We have a fair bit of cash coming in here, one way or the other. People pay cash for tastings. Sometimes they pay cash in the gift shop. Rather take the hit than get the tax people on my back."

"Did he tend to carry a lot of cash?"

"Not as a rule, no. Maybe a couple hundred, that's all."

Quill swallowed another protesting comment. A couple of hundred was a lot of money to her. "What about Mrs. Owens? Did she carry cash around?"

"Her?" Madame made a noise between a "tsk" and a contemptuous "phooey." "You know what I think?"

Quill looked encouraging.

"I think she had something on old Bernie. It's anybody's guess what it was. Maybe found him harassing one of the young girls that waits tables. I'll say this for her, she always had enough to spend. Bernie insisted on a big raise for her just last month. And with the rest of the chefs bellyaching all the time about the quality of her food, I was all for getting rid of her. So there's another suspect for you, Nancy Drew. If it wasn't one of them." She jerked her thumb over her shoulder to the outside. "It was probably Mrs. Owens."

"And Mrs. Owens? Do you have any idea who killed her?"

This time the smile was wide but just as mirthless. "Can't pin that one on me, either. I was having dinner with that mayor of yours. We were whooping it up until one thirty in the morning. As a matter of fact, it was the call from the police about her body being found in Peterson Park that broke the party up."

"I didn't suspect you for a minute," Quill said untruthfully.

"I'm just tickled pink about that," Madame said sarcastically. "Her death wasn't much of a loss. More of a gain, really. You're right about Bernie's death, though. He's going to be almost impossible to replace. Even if I get someone of the quality of your sister. Notice I said almost." Her jaw jutted out. "It may take a while, but I will get someone who can live up to Bernard."

"I sincerely hope you do." Quill's voice

was warm. She had a sudden vision of this woman, friendless, money-mad, with her only reason for happiness a pile of stone and wood.

For the first time, Madame seemed discomfited. Quill didn't think of herself as a fool; she believed in the entire spectrum of human behavior. Most people were decent, and the anger and hostility that came from them originated in fear or a horrible kind of anxiousness that grabbed them by the back of the neck and wouldn't let go. Some people were just plain mean. Not evil-mean, which was another kind of horror altogether, but spiteful, the kind who sincerely enjoyed the small torments they inflicted on others. She wasn't sure about Madame. Who knew what the years of living with LeVasque had done to her? If there was a good woman underneath, now was the time to seek it out.

"I have a favor to ask."

The suspicion was back in her eyes, sudden and hard.

"If you have Mrs. Owens's personal computer, may I have it?"

Madame's shoulders shifted uneasily.

"I desperately want Clare out of jail. I only have one lead in this case and it's incredibly tenuous." Well, there were two, if you counted the fragment of recipe in

LeVasque's hand, but she didn't think a combination of puffed rice and marshmallow was the reason behind two murders. "Mrs. Owens was bent on researching something before she died. There'll be a record of it on her PC."

"What makes you think I have it?"

Quill thought: *It's a matter of your principles, lady. Because you would have taken anything of value out of the poor woman's apartment before the police got there.* But she didn't say it. She didn't say anything at all.

Without a word, Madame got up and went to the massive cherry desk. She unlocked the bottom drawer and took out a little pink PC. Quill had seen that type of computer before. Meg had sent money to an organization that sent them to little kids overseas.

Dorothy set it on the conference table and walked out of the room.

19

Murder will out.
 — "The Prioress's Tale," Chaucer

Quill sat in the gazebo, watching Jack and Bismarck commune in the velvet grass. She'd made it back to the Inn just in time for their four o'clock time together. Mrs. Owens's computer was stuffed in the academy tote at her feet. Bernard LeVasque's face grinned at her, the cheeks bulging out some from the size of the computer behind it. The sun was low across the gorge and touched the copper flashings of the big cream-colored building where the chef had met his death. She'd never been this tired in her life.

"It's not nap time, Mommy!"

"Not yet." She looked at her watch. "Not for another few minutes, yet." Well, there was his supper, but Jack's routines were inviolable.

"So why are you yawning, Mommy!"

"Sorry, darling. Mommy's had a long day. And I swore," she said to Max, who sat beside her with his floppy head on her knees, "that I would never ever be the kind of mother that engaged in Mommy talk. What do you think of that?"

Max cast a nervous eye in the direction of the cat. He went "rrr" low in his throat. It wasn't a growl. In a few minutes, he'd start to talk to her — a series of "rrrs" and modest yowly noises that had the cadence of speech. She'd asked their vet, Dr. McKenzie, about it once. "Imitative of your own speech patterns, my dear," the old man had said briskly. "There's nothing to it. Dogs are pack animals, after all, and if that's what the pack leader does, they're bound to try it, too. Which is not to say" — he'd twinkled at her — "that you can't try to respond in kind."

Quill was prepared to descend to Mommy talk, but she drew the line at "rrr-ing" at her dog. She did say, however, "It's no use being jealous of the cat, Max. If you want to join them, try it. Be nice, though."

Max looked doubtful.

"Maxie!" Jack shouted. "Come and play, Max!"

The doubt in Max's face changed to hope.

"Go on," Quill said. "Nothing ventured and all that good heroic stuff."

Bismarck was on his back, fluffy stomach exposed to the blue sky, his paws draped carelessly over his chest. Max descended the short flight of steps to the grass and stood at the bottom, tail wagging furiously. Bismarck closed his eyes, meditated a long moment, then got up and strolled away.

"The field is yours," Quill said.

Doreen came out of the Tavern Lounge and stamped across the grass. She settled herself beside Quill and joined her in watching Jack throw sticks for the dog. " 'Bout time you got home," she grumbled. "Hear there was a ruckus across there." She jerked her chin at the academy, which was now rosy as the sun sank behind it.

"There was."

"That old coot really leave the place to Meg?"

"Yep."

"And she turned it down?"

"Yep."

"Not without a bit of a struggle, I'll bet."

"Some," Quill admitted.

"Mrs. Peterson wants to see you."

"Mrs. Peterson . . ." Quill broke out of her half-doze. "You mean Marge Schmidt?"

"I mean Marge Schmidt-Peterson," Doreen said firmly. "Says she's found something out real important."

"Well, gosh." Quill got up and looked around. Marge stood at the edge of the flagstone terrace, in uncharacteristic hesitation. "Marge, is anything wrong? Come on over."

"She knows this is your time with Jack," Doreen said in a confidential way. "Didn't want to interfere."

Marge had an air of suppressed excitement. She greeted Quill, accepted the seat Doreen offered her, and looked quite grateful at the idea of a drink. "Vodka, if you don't mind. Tell Nate. He knows how I like it, Doreen. You ought to have one, too, Quill. You're going to need it. Unless . . . ahum." Her eyes darted nervously to Quill's bosom and then to Jack.

"Oh, gosh, no," Quill said. "You stop breast-feeding around six months or so."

"Don't know much about them. Kids, I mean."

"Well, you've certainly met Jack before. Jack, come and say hello to Mrs. Sch . . . I mean Mrs. Peterson, please."

"No," Jack said. "No, no, no."

Quill smacked her head lightly with her palm. "Silly me. Of course. Jack, don't you dare come and say hello to Mrs. Peterson.

Don't even try."

Jack smiled, looking so much like a small, perfect sun in her universe that Quill's heart contracted. He pulled himself up the steps to the gazebo and held out his hand with a cocky air. "Good-bye, Mrs. Peterson. Good-bye. Good-bye."

"I just got here, young man."

"He's the Backward Boy," Quill said. "It's part of being two, which he will be next week. I took a course about it. It's very normal."

"Would you like to meet my lion?" Jack asked.

"A lion?" Marge said with a faint note of alarm. "I don't think I would."

"Then would you like to meet my . . ."

"Here, you," Doreen said. She'd made it to the Tavern Lounge and back in record time. She handed Marge a tall glass of what looked like pure vodka and then hefted Jack onto her hip. "Time for dinner, and then a nap."

"No," Jack said, "no, no, no." He waved over Doreen's shoulder as she carted him back to the Inn. "Hello, Mrs. Peterson. Hello!"

"Bye!" Marge bawled. She creased her brows in bewilderment. "Or do I mean 'hello'? How long does this backward stuff last?"

"Too long. Not long enough. It's terrifying, Marge. He's a different boy every week. But he's always Jack."

"I'll tell you what's terrifying," Marge said with an air of being on familiar ground. "Your near miss with that academy, that's what's terrifying."

"Near miss? I don't get it."

"That LeVasque? Swaggering around like he's the next Warren Buffet? Stone broke."

"Ston . . . you're kidding!"

"I am not." Marge took a healthy swig of her vodka. "Did some checking. Made some calls."

The exact size of Marge's fortune was a cause of considerable speculation in Hemlock Falls. All Quill knew was that any time Marge needed financial background on some poor soul, she got it with a snap of her fingers. And even Quill knew that there were subtly different rules for the hugely wealthy.

"Owes everybody."

"The bank?"

"And then some. It was about to go bust three months ago — and then, all of a sudden, he starts paying things off."

"How?"

"My question exactly. Enterprise like that." Marge narrowed her eyes against the sun and appraised the beautiful building half a mile away. "You're looking at a couple of thousand in revenues a day in season, tops, and next to nothing in the winter. And then you've got overhead . . ."

Quill knew all about overhead. It frequently kept her up at night.

"Anyhow, he starts slinging a hundred K here, a hundred K there at what he owes, and the debt starts to go down."

"An investor, maybe?" Quill hazarded.

Marge pulled at her lower lip. "Possible. Some private deal that doesn't have a paper trail, though."

"Something illegal? Like drugs?"

"Doesn't seem likely. But you never know."

"I had a conversation with Mrs. LeVasque this afternoon."

"Yeah? She have any clue?"

"She didn't give much away." Quill thought back. "She did say her husband seemed to have access to a lot of cash. But she claimed it came from the business."

"We all know about that," Marge said. "Easy to skim when you've got cash coming in like they do. Doesn't make it right. Anyway." She slapped her knees with both hands and got to her feet. "Thought you'd like to know you two aren't as crazy as I thought giving up what looked to be a gold mine."

Quill let this pass. "Are they very close to being bankrupt? It should be working, you know. They're very popular."

"Depends. Not as near as bad off as they were three months ago, that's for sure."

"Thank you, Marge." She stood up to follow her friend inside. "I don't know what this means, exactly, but I'll let you know if I find anything out." She crossed the lawn and stood aside to let Marge precede her into the lounge. "If I can just get some time this evening, we might have a little more information to add to this case."

"Good. That Clare's a decent-enough cook. Shouldn't be spending any more time in the hoosegow than she needs to." She clapped Quill on the shoulder. "I'm off to see to Harland's dinner. Call me if you come up with something."

Quill promised. The tote was an annoying weight on her shoulder, but she was afraid to let the computer out of sight. She hoisted it from her right side to her left and went to check on the evening's activities in the kitchen.

■ ■ ■ ■

"Hey, Quill." Elizabeth Chou stood in Meg's spot at the prep table, her hands deep in a bowl of floury dough.

"Hey yourself. Just dropped in to see if you need any help."

"Nope. It's pretty quiet. I've got gnocchi for the pasta special." She held up her floury hands. "And Bjarne's poaching salmon in something weird."

"Dill coulis is not weird," Bjarne said, mildly. "It is a reduction."

"Right. Anyhow, Dina just brought in the evening's reservations. Six parties of two confirmed."

"And those warped persons," Bjarne said. He filleted a salmon with a neat flick of his wrist. "They love us, I think. And they do not love the Marriott so much."

"Oh, dear," Quill said. "I'm not too happy about that. You know what?" She stood for a long moment, lost in thought.

"What?" Bjarne asked. Then, more loudly, *"What!?"*

Quill jumped. "Nothing. Look. I've got to go to my office and check something out."

She hurried back through the dining room, the tote bumping against her hip. The dining room was beginning to fill up, even though it was fairly early. Quill automatically noticed that the hydrangea in the table vases had been replaced with late roses from the rose garden, and that there was a spot on the blue carpeting that hadn't been there before. "Red wine," Kathleen said as she passed by with a tray of starters. "Might be time to pull it up. I'm telling you, we need to go oak."

Quill agreed in an abstracted way. She crossed into the foyer. Dina sat absorbed in a textbook, one hand on her cheek.

"Hey, Dina."

"Quill!" She closed the text with a snap and followed Quill into her office. "Miriam Doncaster needs to get hold of you. And you know what?"

"What." Quill placed her tote carefully on her desk and just as carefully extracted the computer.

"Cute," Dina said automatically. "I've always liked those things. They're nice and dinky. But the battery sucks. You've got like, forty-five minutes or something, but only if it's fully charged. You have the power cord?"

Quill opened the tote and looked futilely around the contents.

"Bummer," Dina said. "Maybe I can scrounge something. Anyhow, Miriam wants you to call her back right away. And is it true? About the Grouchy Gourmet leaving everything to Meg?"

"He tried to, at any rate. I talked to Howie. Meg has to go through something called Renunciation. That's with a capital 'R' by the way. Anyhow, we do that, and then it's over."

"Hm. Maybe she'll give up flinging sauce pans around, too. Although I'd hate to see it go. It's one of my favorite traditions around here."

"Ha-ha." Quill sat down at her desk and put her palms over her eyes.

"Boy, you look beat," Dina said sympathetically. "Anything I can do? Coffee, maybe? Want me to rub your neck?"

"Yes. No. Maybe. About the coffee, I mean. Are you seeing Davy tonight?"

"Sort of."

"What does that mean? He's going to wave to you as he drives by in his cruiser?"

"It means as soon as the WARPers booked dinner for five tonight, I called him and told him they made you worried sick. So he's coming here. He's going to eat in the dining room at seven thirty, which is when they booked their table, and then I'm going to come and sit with him until they leave or go berserk and try something awful, whichever

307

comes first. I'm off," she said unnecessarily, "at eight."

Quill took her palm from her eyes and stared at her. "I love you, Dina."

"I love you, too, Quill. Now, do you want to call Miriam back? She was so frantic to talk with you I thought she was going to spazz out right over the phone."

Quill looked at her watch. "She'll be at the Croh Bar with Howie."

"Am I that predictable?" Miriam swept into the office. She wore black leather jeans, a man's white cotton shirt (which couldn't have been Howie's; it was too slim-cut), and she had her hair pulled back in a tight French knot at the back of her head.

"You look like Patricia Cornwell," Dina said. "How cool is that?"

Miriam blinked her big blue eyes at them. "I feel *just* like Patricia Cornwell. And I don't want to be late for Howie, so listen up. Bobby Ray Whosis . . ."

"Steinmetz," Quill said.

"Right. He has an alibi. A good one. So they have to let him go."

"What's the alibi?"

Miriam cocked her head and looked at Dina. Everybody in Hemlock Falls knew Dina and the sheriff were dating, and knowing Miriam, odds were good she was the one who'd spread the word. "The police don't seem to have released that, yet."

"I'll say. Davy didn't even tell me." Dina turned to Quill. "Davy only tells me stuff when it's allowed by the department. But," she added earnestly, "he always tells me first."

"Yes, well." Miriam coughed. "The word's all around town that poor Mrs. Whosis, you know, the vic . . ."

"The vic?" Quill said.

"The dead woman," Miriam hissed. She paused impressively. "She had a brand-new fifty-dollar bill clutched in her hand."

"Wow!" Dina said.

"A fifty-dollar bill," Quill repeated. She wasn't as surprised as she thought she'd be. They could call this the Case of the Clutching Corpses. Because poor M. LeVasque had that recipe clutched in his hand, too. Except it had too many "s" sounds in it. The Case of the Corpse That Clutched?

"And that," Miriam said with a grand gesture, "is the clue of the day. If you need me, Watson, you know where to find me." She whirled grandly and made her exit.

"I'm Sherlock!" Quill shouted after her.

"Doesn't sound like much of a clue," Dina said, "unless there's been a robbery somewhere of marked fifty-dollar bills and Mrs.

Owens did it. What are you doing, Quill?"

"Booting up this computer. And I hope to heck the battery's charged. Damn it. It's at fifty percent power. Do you think you can find a power cord that'll fit?"

Dina tipped the little pink case on its side. "I'll try."

Quill's first fear, that the wireless at the Inn wouldn't be compatible with Mrs. Owens's service, proved to be groundless. Her second, that Mrs. Owens's account was password protected proved to be groundless, too. Mrs. Owens had checked the "do not ask for this again" box on her Internet service to save herself the few keystrokes needed to log on.

"Not smart, Mrs. Owens. Not smart at all. But thank goodness, anyway."

She moved the cursor up to the History option. She scrolled down, down, down. The last days of her life, Mrs. Owens had visited a custom shoe site, a holistic vitamin site, and twenty or more cruise ship tours.

Quill kept on scrolling. A red light came on at the corner of the keyboard; 5 percent power left.

Just before the power died Quill hit it.

This Year's Oxbury Grand Prize Winners!

The screen blacked out.

Quill pounded her hands on the desk in

frustration. She wrote the website down, noticing that her hands were trembling, and turned to her own laptop. She logged on quickly, silently blessing the super-speedy service Dina had insisted they sign up for.

The Oxbury Grand Prize was nothing to sneeze at. The cereal company offered a million dollars, cash, to the person who submitted the tastiest recipe using at least four Oxbury products. And this year's winning recipe was for Oxbury's Excellent Krispies.

Coconut Chocolate Marshmallow Mousse

3 cups Oxbury Puffed Rice Cereal

1 cup Oxbury Fine Spun Sugar

3 tablespoons Oxbury Fine Ground Cake Flour

1 package Oxbury Pillow-Soft Marshmallows

2 2/3 cups Oxbury coconut

2 cups butter

6 eggs

2 cups heavy cream

Along with cinnamon, chocolate, walnuts, and vanilla

They had posted the winner's face, of course.

Mrs. Barbarossa.

Quill paged down the website, a little dizzy with shock. Mrs. Barbarossa's real name was Serena Owens Canfield. Under the picture of the triumphant little old lady was an interview with the Oxbury judges. She had a sister, Verena Owens, who was a professional chef, but the two hadn't seen each other for years, and of course Mrs. Owens (the older by ten minutes) hadn't a thing to do with the winning recipe.

But Quill bet Bernard LeVasque had.

"Quill?"

Absorbed in the screen, Quill didn't register the fear in Dina's voice at first. She looked up and for a long, horrifying moment, what she saw didn't register at all.

"That damn website," Mrs. Barbarossa said. She held Dina's left arm high behind her back. Her other hand, shining with rings, held a long, thin boning knife against Dina's neck. The front of Dina's T-shirt was soaked with blood. "I demanded that they take it off, but they said they had the right to leave it up for a year. For the publicity."

Quill got up, slowly.

"I asked in the dining room if anyone had a power cord to match your little pink computer cord." Dina managed a ghastly smile. "She said she had one just like it."

"Shut up." Mrs. Barbarossa pressed the

knife closer against Dina's neck and a little stream of blood flowed over the old lady's knuckles. It didn't take much pressure. Boning knives were lethally sharp. "Vee and I bought matching computers at the same time," she said chattily. "Right after I won the contest. She lost hers on a cruise ship and didn't get herself another one until a couple of days ago. Funny how much these things get hold of you. Who'd have thought we'd cotton on to computers at our age?"

Quill moved carefully away from her desk.

"That's right," Mrs. Barbarossa said. "I want you to go out and go upstairs. I need that nice little boy of yours. I can't drive through the countryside with this great gawk of a girl in the car."

"Not Jack!" Dina said. "I'll go with you!" Her face was so pale, Quill was afraid she was going to faint.

"I wouldn't hurt a hair on his head! What kind of a person do you think I am?"

Quill moved away from the desk, step-by-step. "A very clever person, to be sure," she said steadily.

"Well, I have been smarter than the average bear," she said coyly. "You just go on up now and get little Jack. The two of us will wait right here." She bared her teeth. "If you don't go right this minute, I'll pull this knife all the way across her throat and be out that window before you know it."

"Of course you will," Quill said. "But you'll want to take your sister's computer. It's evidence. And you wouldn't want the police to get their hands on it. Vee, is it? And the two of you are sisters?"

"Thank God I got the looks. We never got along all that well, to tell you the truth."

"She didn't seem like a very nice person." By now, Quill was three feet from them. She held the computer out, like an offering. She held Dina's eyes with hers and shook her head lightly. *No*

"Well, she wasn't," Mrs. Barbarossa said fretfully. "Do you know, she wanted to take my money, too?"

"Just like Chef LeVasque."

"That man! He thought the recipe was a joke! Vee tried to make the recipe herself, you know." Mrs. Barbarossa sniffed contemptuously. "And the little jackass said he could win it in a snap. But the two of them are professionals. They aren't eligible."

"So it was really LeVasque's recipe? And not yours, after all?"

Mrs. Barbarossa took an indignant breath. Quill raised the computer and swung hard. Dina, weak with fear, shoved herself sideways. Quill cracked the old lady on the

314

head, driven by panic for Jack, for Dina, and filled with horror at herself.

Mrs. Barbarossa went down like a stone.

Quill grabbed the knife and threw it out the open window. Dina sat dazed on the floor. Quill grabbed her by the shoulders and cradled her against her breast. She pulled off her shirt and wrapped it around the wounds in Dina's neck, then laid her carefully flat on the floor. She opened the door and shouted for Davy. Then she punched 911 frantically into the phone and shouted for the paramedics. She sat down again, Dina in her arms, half-naked, covered with blood, weeping.

20

Academy Welcomes New Chef!
— Headline from the
Hemlock Falls Gazette,
August 14th

"She was as crazy as an outhouse rat," Meg said wonderingly. "How in the world did she think she could get away with it?"

The sun was dropping behind the academy across the gorge. Less than twenty-four hours had passed since the paramedics had taken Dina and Mrs. Barbarossa to the emergency room. Meg and Quill sat in the gazebo. Doreen sat on the steps, silent.

Jack was asleep on Quill's lap. She'd had to leave him with Doreen to give her official statement to the police, but she hadn't let him out of her sight once she'd gotten back to the Inn.

"I don't know how I'd have lived with myself if I'd killed her, Meg."

"Well, you didn't," Meg said. "And nobody would have blamed you if you had. What else could you do?"

Quill smoothed Jack's curls. "Maybe not hit her so hard." She'd felt sick with dread all day.

"Don't think about it."

"I can't stop thinking about it!"

"She killed two people, Quill. She would have killed poor Dina without a second thought. She threatened you."

"She wouldn't have gotten near Jack," Quill said fiercely. "I don't like knowing this about myself, Meg. That I can do what I did."

"I like knowing it," Meg said. "You were brave. And you were in a corner. And like the man said, you did what you had to do."

"What man?"

"I don't know. *The* Man. What, you were supposed to stand there and let her cut Dina's throat? Just so you could avoid clocking a monster over the head with a computer?" She reached over and tucked a curl behind Quill's ear. "Your hair's falling down again."

Jack stirred in her arms, woke, and sat up. Then he began to wriggle. "Let me down, Mommy."

"Not just yet, Jack."

"Yes, just yet! Let me down *now!*" He held out his arms to Doreen. *"Gram!"* he shouted. "Mommy's squishing me!"

Doreen got to her feet with a grunt. "You'd best let me take him up for dinner."

Quill put her cheek against Jack's. He smelled of sunshine, soap, and little boy.

Doreen's face softened. "Best to keep to his routine, dear. It's all over now."

"You're right."

Quill let him down. He scrambled off her lap and danced out of the gazebo and into the sunshine. "Chase me, Gram."

"I'm too old and too cranky to go off a-chasing you," Doreen said sternly. "You get up on to bed, now. As for you two," she put her hands on her hips. "You'd best come on in and eat something. You haven't had a thing all day, Quill. And as for you, missy, you've got some free time on your hands — you can spend it making something tasty for your sister."

Quill clapped her hand to her head. "The Welcome Dinner! I forgot all about it! Shouldn't you be at the academy?"

"Cancelled," Doreen said. "So she's free as a bird. I'm taking Jack up, now, and I'll look in on Dina."

"Don't wake her up," Quill warned. "Andy Bishop prescribed a sedative for her. I finally got her to take it. The more she rests, the faster she'll heal."

"She's going to have a right good scar," Doreen predicted gloomily. "But at least her head's still attached to her neck. Wouldn't have been if it hadn't been for you, Quill." She touched Quill's cheek with a gnarled finger. "I'm proud to know you, missy. You did the right thing."

The heaviness in Quill's heart lightened, just a little.

"As for that Welcome Dinner, Meg will tell you all about that. Goat!" She turned and trudged across the lawn after Jack.

Quill raised her eyebrows. "Goat?"

"Nobody wanted goat." Meg settled comfortably back into the lounge chair. "We had exactly three confirmed guests. Once the word got out about the entree, people stayed away in droves. Of course, the hoorah here had something to do with it, too." There was a cynical twist to her mouth. "We'd be full up tonight if I hadn't closed the kitchen."

"It wouldn't have been anyone from Hemlock Falls," Quill said warmly.

"No," Meg agreed. "But the media's not prone to either tact or respect. I've got Mike posted at the end of the driveway in the pickup."

"I didn't think of that. That was smart."

"Glad it meets with your approval. So." Meg moved restlessly in her chair. "Did Davy let you in on the particulars?"

"Some. Mrs. Barbarossa — it's Serena Canfield, actually, started paying blackmail money to LeVasque about a month after she got all that cash."

"So it was his recipe."

"Yes, it was. The contest has strict rules about professionals, of course. Only amateurs. And Serena claims that once the news about her win was publicized, all kinds of people came out of the woodwork demanding money from her."

"I've heard that happens to people who win the lottery."

"It's one of the reasons a lot of state lotteries let you opt for anonymity. Anyhow, Serena's quite the blogger. She met a few other lottery winners online and came up with the idea for this group."

"WARP."

"It stands for Winners Against Rapacious Predators."

"Oh, my."

"That was Collier's contribution, by the way. The name."

"The mortgage banker?"

"Ironic, no?"

"Very."

They grinned at each other.

Quill was feeling better and better. "They formed this group and elected Serena president. Her gruesome little joke was that they all take the names of dead lottery winners. All of them wanted to change their names, because every single winner had the same problem. Demands for money from relatives, friends, and strangers.

"Anyhow, Serena decided she'd had enough of LeVasque's demands. So she arranged this little convention here at the Inn."

"She planned to kill him all along?"

"Apparently."

"The state of New York isn't going to like that."

"Premeditated, without a doubt. So, she killed him." Quill took a deep breath. "This is an even uglier part. Vee . . ."

"That's Mrs. Owens."

"Vee decided she had a right to some of the money, too. After all, she was the one who'd passed the winning recipe along to her sister. And Serena had had enough. She'd given LeVasque more than four hundred thousand dollars, the state and the feds had taken a bunch for taxes, and she had jewelry bills to pay."

"You mean those rhinestone brooches?"

"Weren't rhinestones at all."

"Golly."

"Yep. A jewel and her money are soon parted."

Meg groaned.

"Bobby Ray Steinmetz was the obvious person to take the fall for Vee's murder. He had a record, and he was going through his lottery winnings at a rapid rate, so Serena figured the police would find a motive if somehow the robbery part came out."

"She met Vee at the statue in Peterson Park to hand over more cash. And after she killed her, she took it back."

"How did she get her hands on the knife from my kitchen?"

"Sheer bad luck for Clare. I don't think LeVasque actually meant to steal it, Meg. But you were chasing him around the prep table with the sauté pan, and I think he just grabbed it with some muddled idea of defending himself. He left it in the kitchens at the academy and Serena picked it up because it was the biggest, heaviest knife on the rack. She told Davy she wanted to make sure she did the job right."

"So poor Clare . . ."

"Should be out of jail as soon as Justin can get the proper paperwork done."

"Then she'll be home for dinner," Meg said with an irritating air of complacency. "Justin's a genius."

It took more than a few hours to get Clare out of the Five Points Correctional Facility, but she walked into the Tavern Lounge with Justin late Saturday afternoon looking worn, too thin, and happy.

"Hey!" Meg leaped out of her chair and hugged her. "You're free!"

"You'd think it'd be like the movies," Clare said wryly. "You find the real murderer and boom! You're presented with the jailhouse key. Doesn't work like that."

"Process," Justin said with a half smile. He put his arm around Meg and kissed the top of her head. "Are we in time?"

"We haven't started yet."

"What's with all the balloons?" Clare said. "Is it somebody's birthday?"

"Mine!" Jack said. "I'm two!" He proudly put three fingers up. He held a stuffed rabbit by one ear. Max trailed after him. Bismarck trailed after Max. The cat took a long look at his mistress, then strolled up and twined around her ankles. Clare bent down and rubbed his head. "I missed you, too, buddy."

"That is my lion," Jack said. "And that is

my birthday cake. And that is my mommy."
He cocked his head to one side. "All of my
friends are here." He pointed. "That's Dina.
She hurt her neck. But it's going to be okay,
Mommy says. That's Davy, her good friend.
He is helping her with her neck."

"Because his arm is around her?" Clare
guessed.

"Exactly. And there are my friends from
the kitchen, too. And Mike. Mike is a good
digger, but not as good as I am."

"And your gram, of course." Clare waved
at Doreen.

"Yes." He clapped his hands in delight.
"They are all here for my birthday! It's
because I'm two!"

"You are a fortunate boy," Clare agreed.
She stiffened. "My God. Is that Madame?"

Quill glanced over at the corner table.
Mrs. LeVasque sat between Harland and
Marge. Harland looked mildly grumpy.
(What sixty-two-year-old dairy farmer
wants to be at a birthday party for a two-
year-old boy? Quill had seen that he was
well supplied with beer.) Marge listened at-
tentively to Madame. All three of them
turned and looked at Clare.

"There's an opening at the academy,"
Quill said. "Madame was hoping you'd be
interested. And your old rooms at the an-

nex are ready for you and Bismarck." She paused. "Meg and I persuaded her that the employment contract you had with LeVasque should have been voided by his death."

"So you're free to choose." Meg put her hands on her hips. "What I'm thinking is that the two of us working together can come up with pretty fabulous ideas to keep the tourists coming to both places. What about it."

Clare turned perfectly white. Then a tide of red swept up from her collarbone to her hairline. "I don't owe anybody any money anymore."

"Let me sort those 'any's' out." Meg closed her eyes. "Hmm. The answer would be no, you don't owe anyone a thing."

"And I've got a job?"

"If you want it."

Clare pinched her nose hard, but two tears ran down her cheeks. "I owe you," she said. "If I can think of a way to thank you . . . there's no way to thank you."

"Sure there is." Meg grabbed her by the arm. "About that recipe for the short-bread . . ."

"Meg," Quill said.

"So never mind about the recipe for the shortbread."

"I can't quite take all this in," Clare

admitted. "I think I'm dreaming."

Meg grabbed her arm. "C'mon. You'll be right across the gorge from us. It'll be cool." She dragged Clare over to the table. Justin grabbed Meg's free hand and followed them. Quill watched them and tried not to feel incredibly sentimental.

Jack tugged imperatively at Quill's skirt. "Daddy."

"I know, darling. I miss him, too."

"Daddy!" Jack pulled at her skirt and she turned around.

There he was, standing in the doorway. His hair was a little grayer around the temples. There were a few more lines around his coin-colored eyes. And he was darkly tanned from some desert sun thousands of miles away.

"Myles," she said.

He opened his arms and she went into them.

AUTHOR'S NOTE

I'm absolutely delighted to be bringing the next volume of Meg and Quill's adventures in Hemlock Falls to readers. If you have met Meg and Quill before, I'd like to say, welcome back! And if you are new to this series, thank you very much for giving us a try.

If you have a love for cooking, I would love to hear from you. Join me for a chat any time on my blog at www.claudia bishop.com/blog. I'm especially interested in kitchen experiences.

Q: What is your main purpose when you create a menu?

Q: Has the way you've cooked changed over the years?

Q: Where did you learn your way around the kitchen?

Q: Do you have a favorite technique? What gives you the most pleasure at the stove?

Q: How important is equipment? The oven? What tools are essential to you?

ABOUT THE AUTHOR

Claudia Bishop has authored many mysteries under her name and the name Mary Stanton, and is the senior editor of three mystery anthologies. She divides her time between a working farm in upstate New York and a small home in Florida.